MONSTER MOVIE!

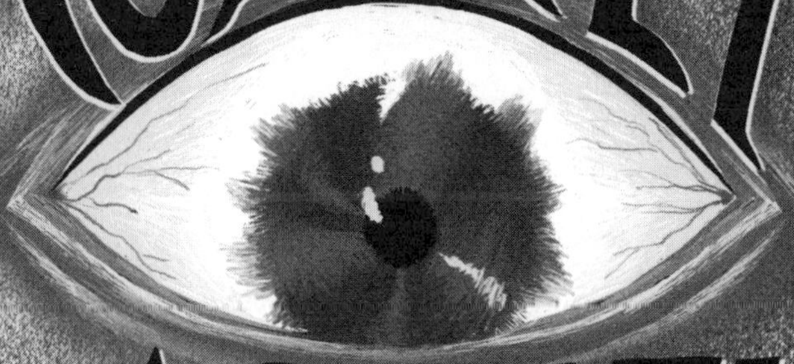

CHUCK WENDIG

LITTLE, BROWN AND COMPANY
NEW YORK BOSTON

This book is a work of fiction. Names, characters, places, and incidents are the product of the author's imagination or are used fictitiously. Any resemblance to actual events, locales, or persons, living or dead, is coincidental.

Copyright © 2024 by Terribleminds LLC

Interior art credits: Title page art and lettering © 2024 by George Ermos; noise texture © Billion Photos/Shutterstock.com; theater marquee © hugolacasse/Shutterstock.com; background art for part openers © Callahan/Shutterstock.com; film strip © Kobee/Shutterstock.com; tv vector © Ivan Dubovik/Shutterstock.com; siren emoji © Cosmic_Design/Shutterstock.com

Cover art copyright © 2024 by George Ermos. Cover design by Jenny Kimura.
Cover copyright © 2024 by Hachette Book Group, Inc.
Interior design by Jenny Kimura.

Hachette Book Group supports the right to free expression and the value of copyright. The purpose of copyright is to encourage writers and artists to produce the creative works that enrich our culture.

The scanning, uploading, and distribution of this book without permission is a theft of the author's intellectual property. If you would like permission to use material from the book (other than for review purposes), please contact permissions@hbgusa.com. Thank you for your support of the author's rights.

Little, Brown and Company
Hachette Book Group
1290 Avenue of the Americas, New York, NY 10104
Visit us at LBYR.com

First Edition: September 2024

Little, Brown and Company is a division of Hachette Book Group, Inc. The Little, Brown name and logo are registered trademarks of Hachette Book Group, Inc.

The publisher is not responsible for websites (or their content)
that are not owned by the publisher.

Little, Brown and Company books may be purchased in bulk for business, educational, or promotional use. For information, please contact your local bookseller or the Hachette Book Group Special Markets Department at special.markets@hbgusa.com.

Library of Congress Cataloging-in-Publication Data
Names: Wendig, Chuck, author.
Title: Monster movie! / Chuck Wendig.
Description: First edition. | New York : Little, Brown and Company, 2024. | Audience: Ages 8–12. | Summary: Twelve-year-old Ethan is afraid of everything, but he must overcome his fears to save his town from a cursed videotape turned monster on the loose.
Identifiers: LCCN 2023054605 | ISBN 9780316572590 (hardcover) | ISBN 9780316572613 (ebook)
Subjects: CYAC: Video tapes—Fiction. | Monsters—Fiction. | Friendship—Fiction. | Middle schools—Fiction. | Schools—Fiction. | City and town life—Fiction. | Horror stories. | Humorous stories. | LCGFT: Monster fiction. | Horror fiction. | Humorous fiction. | Novels.
Classification: LCC PZ7.W469133 Mo 2024 | DDC [Fic]—dc23
LC record available at https://lccn.loc.gov/2023054605

ISBNs: 978-0-316-57259-0 (hardcover), 978-0-316-57261-3 (ebook)

Printed in Indiana, USA

LSC-C

Printing 1, 2024

TO MY MOTHER, WHO LET ME RENT MY FIRST SCARY MOVIE. (SPOILER WARNING, IT WAS *ALIEN*, I WAS PROBABLY TOO YOUNG FOR IT, OOPS.)

PART ONE

DON'T LOSE YOUR HEAD, ETHAN PITOWSKI

ONE
MISTER CHITTERS MAKES A CALL

"SO THERE IT IS," HARLEY Wurth said, pointing out the window of his bedroom, past the overhanging roof, toward a big-trunked pine tree. It was Sunday, and he had texted both Ethan and Olivia an hour ago:

> HUMONGOUS ELEPHANT FORSYTHIA

They knew what their secret code meant, so they headed right over, and now they were looking out the window with him.

Harley had a big goofy smile on his face. (Because he always did. Olivia said he was definitely the reincarnated spirit of a golden retriever. That felt true to Ethan.)

Ethan—that is to say, Ethan Pitowski, who lived a

mile away, on the other end of Main Street—squinted into the sun. "I don't see it." He let his gaze drift past the tree, down to the narrow, bumpy sidewalk. The houses on this side of town were older: Victorians that gave way to ranch-style homes. On Ethan's side of town, the sidewalks were straighter and wider, and the houses were of a style his mother called "craftsman." She often said that the Victorians and the craftsmans didn't really get along—some stylistic battle of old versus new, tired versus modern, both in terms of money and how long they'd lived there. Don't even get her started on the ranch-style homes, either. Ethan didn't understand any of it. Adults were weird. "Sorry, Harley. Are you sure it's in the tree?"

"Oh, it's there," Harley said, using both hands to hook bits of his raggedy blond mullet around his oversize ears. "I swear."

"Yeah, I don't see it either," Olivia James said. Harley was tall, but Olivia was even taller—she, a Black girl with big purple glasses and Invisalign braces, was all legs and all arms and a puff of hair that only extended her height.

Ethan had an idea. "Maybe send it a text?"

"On it," Olivia said. She pulled out her phone and said, "Open the window so we can hear."

Harley shrugged, then opened it, grunting. He seemed to take a moment to enjoy the late spring breeze blowing in, making a little *mm* sound. Ethan almost expected his tongue to loll out of his mouth like a dog with its head out the car window.

Olivia used her phone to text Harley's.

Sure enough, out there in the pine tree—

Ding-doo-ding

At that, Ethan finally saw the phone tucked in the crook of two branches. The screen glowed for a minute and then dimmed again.

Olivia saw it too.

"Can't you just climb back out there and get it?" she asked Harley. "I mean, you put it there."

Harley shrugged again. "Oh yeah, no, I didn't put it out there."

Blink, blink. Ethan felt crazy for asking, but he had to. "So...how, exactly, did it get into the tree?"

"Oh! Haha, yeah. Mister Chitters took it."

Olivia and Ethan shared a *what exactly is Harley talking about now* kind of look. This was a regular occurrence. Because, well. Harley was Harley.

"Mister Chitters," Olivia said, repeating the words in a low tone. Incredulous. Dubious. *Most uncertain.*

"Haha, yeah, he's my squirrel friend."

Another look. Another round of *blink blink blink*. "You have a squirrel friend?" Ethan asked, twitching a little. A tiny anxiety bubble appeared in his mind, threatening to swell and then go *pop*.

"Totally." Harley itched the armpit of his shirt, which displayed art for a band called Demongallop. It showed a horse with demon horns riding a spiky electric guitar. Ethan didn't like it. "We hang out sometimes."

"I don't think he's much of a friend if he stole your phone," Olivia said.

"He just got confused because of the peanut butter."

Conversations with Harley were sometimes like riding a roller coaster designed by a five-year-old who's gone goofy on energy drinks. In the middle of a hurricane.

Olivia was done being polite. "Harley, just spit it out!"

"Oh, okay. Yeah, so sometimes I sit here by the window and watch Mister Chitters, and then *sometimes* I open the window and we, like, hang out and stuff, and I tell Mister Chitters my problems and Mister Chitters chitters his problems at me and it's real cool, and then one time I was like, *Aw, man, I bet you're hungry, Mister C*, and so I went downstairs and got some peanut butter and put it on my phone like a little plate, and I served it to him and he seemed to really, really like it, like, *a lot*, but then when he was done? He took the plate."

"The plate...being your phone."

"That's right."

"And why didn't you use, like, a spoon?"

"Because I knew my mom wouldn't want me using one of our spoons," he said, as if that made all the sense in the world.

Ethan could not contain his squick at this point. He kept it calm at first: "Harley, you shouldn't be that close to a wild animal. They have *diseases*. Did you know that marmots carry the Plague? You know? *The Black Death*."

Uh-oh. He found himself speaking faster and faster, a burbling babble of *ahhhhhhhHHHHH*. But it was impossible to slow down.

"Don't even get me *started* on rabies. So who *knows* what kind of diseases squirrels have. And now that thing has touched your phone, and—and—" His brain raced, and he was imagining that Harley was the vector for some weird *squirrel-human hybrid* disease, and that they were all *sucking in tainted squirrel breath*, and he felt his breathing quicken and his pulse race and—

It was Harley and Olivia's turn to share a look. They had a patented *Ethan* look just like Ethan and Olivia had a *Harley* one.

"Dude," Olivia said. "You're spiraling."

"A little," Ethan said, almost gasping.

"C'mere," she said, beckoning him closer. Then she did the thing where she got up alongside him and pushed her shoulder against his—like she was a tree he could lean on. And he did. "You're good," she said.

"It's cool, man. Mister Chitters doesn't have diseases, probably," Harley blurted out. "He's just nuts for peanuts—hahaha! Get it? Because nuts? Though I don't think peanuts are nuts. They're legumes. Shoot. And I don't think there are any good legume jokes." Jokes were his way of offering reassurance. While Ethan was sure everything was going to go utterly wrong all the time, Harley was the opposite: certain that things would work out, no worries, it'll be fine to jump into this quarry, or to eat those weird berries, or to ramp a skateboard over that beehive. "Anyway! I just want my phone back."

Ethan tried to calm his panic attack. He had techniques. Being with his friends helped. Olivia's voice and presence were good for this sort of thing. She steadied him.

"Okay," he said, nodding. "Okay."

"Awesome," Harley said. "So I was thinking, like, I'd just take a running jump off the roof and grab the phone, and you guys could hang out at the bottom of the tree and catch me after."

"*Ennnh*," Olivia said, again dubious. "Ethan, you wanna take this?"

Ethan shook his head, anxiety ramping right back

up. "No! No. *No*. Harley, that is not a plan, that is a guaranteed admission to the hospital. You can't just jump into a tree! You'll break things! An arm! A leg! The very crucial *neck*!"

"I dunno," Harley said, pronouncing it *eye-unno*. "I'm nimble."

(Spoiler warning: He was not nimble.)

"Nah," Olivia said. "You're not. Ethan's right, Har. Bad idea. We will *not* be able to catch you. But I got a better idea." To Ethan she said, "You got your notebook?"

He nodded. It was as reliable as rain that Ethan had his notebook on him.

"Start to draw this—"

Except, interruption. Suddenly the door opened and Harley's dad came in. He was like an inflated, swollen version of Harley. Taller, wider, not muscly so much as marshmallowy. He, too, had a mullet: His was a well-washed chestnut color. He wore a tie-dye sleeveless T-shirt and cargo shorts, despite it being spring and still a little chilly out.

"'Sup, kids, whatcha doing?" Mr. Wurth asked.

"Just trying to rescue my phone out of the tree because a squirrel took it," Harley said.

"Oh, gnarly," the dad said, with no further questions. "Have fun."

"Wait," Olivia called out. "Mr. Wurth, do you have, like, a bungee cord?"

"Sure. I use a bunch in my trailer." Harley's dad always had junk around—buying it, selling it, transporting it. "I'll grab a few."

At that, Olivia began instructing Ethan on how to draw her plan—basically, they were going to create a swing out of bungee cords and, from the corner of the roof, swing Harley over to the tree. Ethan furiously sketched this out—he was pretty proud of how much Harley looked like Harley, even though he was a little kawaii cartoon version. (His big mullety bucket head in particular was pretty perfect, Ethan decided.) He felt himself calming down, returning to normal, enjoying the peace that drawing brought him.

"Aw, man, looks cool," came a voice over Ethan's shoulder, and he nearly peed his pants. It was just Mr. Wurth, though, having come back in with the bungee cords. "Looks like fun, too."

It was unsurprising that Mr. Wurth was just as excited about this plan as Harley—Harley's father was famous for once getting his meaty hand stuck in a pickle jar. He got it out by doing a karate punch against the countertop. (He had to get seven stitches, a fact he thought was "pretty rad, huh?") That was just one of his many misadventures. The phrase *like father, like son* hadn't made much sense to Ethan before he met the Wurth family, but now he had to wonder.

So if Harley was on board with Olivia's plan, and Harley's *father* was on board, that meant this was very clearly a bad idea.

Ethan felt himself poised to spiral again.

"Okay. No. Okay. We're not—we're *not* doing this." He started scribbling hasty doodles of the potential dangers. "Harley could fall, break a leg." There, a snapped stick figure leg emitting little lightning-bolt pain lines. "He could impale himself on a branch." Stick Figure Harley now had a tree branch emerging from his stick figure heart. "He could get the bungee cord wrapped around his ankle and smack into the side of the house, and then he'd just be dangling and...and...I don't know, a deer could attack him!" Stick Figure Harley dangled on the page, speared by the many-pointed antlers of Stick Figure Deer.

Harley said, with utter seriousness, "It would be an honor to be attacked by a deer. They're so *majestic*."

"Ethan, I think the plan is good—" Olivia started to say, but Ethan interrupted with another objection.

"Not to mention the *sap*." This he didn't even bother to draw. "Pine trees are gooey with sap, and that stuff does not come off with regular soap. What if Harley gets stuck to the tree and can never ever get *un*stuck—"

"Ethan—"

"Wait."

Hold up.

Sap.

Sticky.

He did a quick scan of Harley's room, which was of course a mess—a chaos bomb of clothes in piles and a half-assembled drum kit and LEGO bricks left around like caltrops. But there on the wall, next to a Demongallop poster, was a kid's bow-and-arrow set.

"That's it," he said.

Everyone leaned in, as if to silently ask, *What's it?*

Ethan grinned and began to draw.

TWO
MISSION: MOSTLY POSSIBLE

IT TOOK THEM A WHILE. Mr. Wurth watched, rapt, as they tied the bungee cord to the arrow and got a little tree sap to apply to the arrow's suction-cup tip. (Kids were not supposed to play with sharp arrows, a fact that both Harley *and* his father seemed to find disagreeable.) Then they each took shots at the phone. Ethan knew he was going to get a blister or accidentally put out his eye with a sap-smeared arrow, and his shot went wide as he winced. Harley was impatient enough that he never really lined up his shot, so the arrow stuck to the trunk and they had to tug it free. Olivia, on the other hand, was as cool as an open refrigerator on a hot summer day and stayed steady-handed and stock-still. Her first arrow flew true, hitting the phone in the crook of the branches. *Fwud!*

And it stuck! They reeled in the phone, then celebrated their triumph with popcorn and Reese's Peanut Butter Cups. Harley didn't even care that his phone was sticky, maybe forever. You know. Because of the sap.

They had a good thing going, these three friends, but Ethan sometimes felt like he didn't fit in with them. Olivia was cool and confident. Harley wasn't confident so much as he just didn't think too hard about anything and, like any good golden retriever, would run instantly toward danger to help a friend (or if it looked fun). And then there was Ethan. Ethan, the secret artist, because his parents didn't want him to be an artist. Ethan, who was not confident at all, but permanently uncertain and entirely scared of everything and everyone in the world. Except his friends. He wasn't scared of them.

On days like today, when their plan came together and they had fun doing it, their group made sense. Olivia always told Ethan, "That's your thing, dude. You keep us real. Harley wants to do everything and I think I can do anything, but you keep our feet on the ground."

He was glad to have a role, but he knew he wasn't exactly the most awesome kind of friend to hang out with—he felt like a boat anchor, the person who keeps you down, the friend who reminds you that maybe you *can't* do something, the pal who describes in nattering detail all your limitations and how if you're not careful, you'll get eaten by a shark or get tetanus or catch some weird squirrel disease.

But today, at least, their friendship worked.

Tomorrow, Monday, back at school—well, that would bring a new set of worries, wouldn't it?

THREE
NEVER TRUST A CROWD

MONDAY. SCHOOL. RECESS.

Wandering outside, Ethan saw the group of kids gathering at the picnic benches behind the big green wooden wall on the school playground—a group that seemed to be growing by the moment. Kids were being summoned by the mere presence of other kids, as if the group were a planetoid mass with increasing gravity, the crowd swelling with pairs and trios of friends and enemies alike, cliques and clumps and the rare loner. And to this Ethan said, *Nope, no chance*, and turned to walk back the other way.

(After all, those kids were probably full of germs. They might have mice in their pockets, or snakes, and mice could have hantavirus, and snakes might carry salmonella. And even if none of that was true, Ethan did not want to bother any of the kids by being near them, or looking weird, or acting weird, or bumping into someone. He hoped not to draw their ire or, honestly, their attention at all. Life was just...easier that way.)

Except, then he heard it:

"Dude. Dude! *Dude.*"

It was Olivia calling to him from *within the crowd*. She was easy to see, given that she was taller than all of them.

She summoned Ethan with a swishing arm.

Ethan shook his head stiffly. *No, mm-mm, uh-uh.*

"DUDE," she said, the word hissed through her braces.

Then Harley popped up next to her like a happy groundhog, his face cut in half by a big goofy smile. He waved Ethan closer too, bellowing for Ethan because Harley had no chill.

"Ethan! Yo! Ethan! Ethan! Hey! Hey, man! Hey! Ethan! Hey! *C'mere!*"

Now a few looks drifted toward Ethan. The gazes of other children pinned him like beams from Superman's eyes, and Ethan felt warmer and warmer, like he was on fire under their *scrutinous* stares.

And that was how Ethan ended up caught in the group's gravity too. Summoned by the power of the crowd, drawn like a magnet to a magnet. He wished instead to be repelled, to be pushed away and cast to the margins.

AHHHHH, he thought, screaming internally, as he headed toward the gathering kids, his gut curdling like milk and lemonade.

As Ethan joined Olivia and Harley, he heard the voice of Kevin Rook. The richest kid in the sixth grade was holding court.

"—yeah, you know the Monarch Theater, the one down on Belkin Street? Yeah, the one that closed down. I know the manager. He hooked me up."

Billy Senf, a little dark-haired, dark-eyed kidney stone of a boy, piped up: "Is it *really* that scary?"

Kevin Rook, who sat not on the bench of the picnic table but on the table itself, bit into a chonky triangle of Toblerone chocolate. "Eh, I haven't watched it yet. But it's supposed to not just be kinda scary—it's supposed to be the *scariest movie ever made*. People, like, *freaked* in the theater when it came out forever ago. They all yarfed and slipped around on their yarf, and then they passed out in their own yack and, like, had to go into therapy after."

Rachel Malinenko, the richest girl in class, nodded knowingly, because there was no arena in which she did not claim *total supreme expertise*, and said, "Yup, it's true.

People died. They went to the theater, and they were so scared by this movie, their hearts basically exploded like Mentos in Diet Coke. *Boosh.*"

The crowd gasped collectively. A murmur of shock passed through them like an electric current.

Ethan didn't know what was going on, but he liked precisely none of it.

He tried to squirm away, sneaking back out through the crowd—

—but Olivia fishhooked him under the armpit and pulled him back in.

Harley leaned toward Ethan and said in a whispered voice way too loud and unwhispery, "Kevin got a copy of *Demons of Death 4: Death Fingers*, and he's gonna play it this Friday night at his house."

"Everybody is invited," Olivia said, her face aglow with the possibility. *"Ev-er-ee-bod-ee."*

"Cool," Ethan said, forcing a toothy smile and an awkward thumbs-up.

Again he tried to extract himself.

And again Olivia dragged him back.

The gravity of crowds, he thought. *Ugh ugh ugh aahhhhhh.*

Other questions arose from the teeming mass of sixth graders as Ethan tucked in his arms and tried not to sweat, which only made him sweat more.

"Is it, like, streaming or whatever?"

Kevin Rook: "Nah, it's a tape. An old-timey VCR tape."

At this, the kids all looked askance at one another with something approaching a perfect combination of wonder and disgust. This spawned a momentary conversation about how people used to watch movies on big ugly tapes instead of with the click of a button or swipe of their finger, and then one kid said something about how his dad still collected something called "laser discs" and how cool *that* sounded. Eventually Kevin Rook told them all to shut up, and they got back to talking about the scariest scary movie.

"Do we have to watch the first three movies before this one?"

Kevin Rook: "What? No. Who cares?"

(To this, an echo from the crowd in agreement. *Yeah, duh, who cares?*)

"Are your parents going to be home?"

Kevin Rook, grinning like a cat: "I'm gonna show the movie on *parent-engagement night*." On that phrase, *parent-engagement night*, Kevin Rook did a bit of a theatrical hand flourish. (While his father was some kind of super-important business guy, his mother was once a

Broadway actress.) "All our parents will be *here* learning about stupid volunteering garbage and community barf and PTA blah...while all of *us* will be at *my* house. Watching the freakiest, frightiest, poop-your-pantsiest movie you little milk babies have *ever seen*."

FOUR
THE SCAREDIEST CAT EVER BORN

AS NOTED, ETHAN PITOWSKI WAS scared of pretty much everything.

This, to Ethan, was just good sense. The world was bonkers. Legit cuckoo bananapants bonkers. Sure, you had your *classic*, obvious things to be afraid of: dog bites, open manhole covers, creepy vans, various funguses. But if you went ahead and scratched the paint off human existence, it was easy to find an unholy host of horrible potential outcomes. He'd read a story where a chunk of frozen bodily waste fell off the bottom of a commercial airliner and punched a hole through a suburban house like a meteor made of frosty poop and icy pee. Or...or... did you know that sometimes space junk, like old satellites, could fall on your head? It went up, and eventually it had to come down. Randomly. Space junk might just crater the bus on the way to school one day. Or...or...*or*, there were parasites. Tiny worms. Itty-bitty bugs. Microscopic paramecia and bacteria and what was the other thing? Amoebas! So many amoebas! *Too* many amoebas! They just wanted to get in your brain and take it over and turn it to goo, like in a horror movie.

Maybe even in *the* horror movie.

The one Kevin Rook planned to show to all the sixth graders—

At least, to those who showed up.

But Ethan would not show up to Kevin Rook's house on Friday night. Not Friday night, not next week, not in a million years.

He was definitely, certainly, absolutely *not* going.

FIVE
A SLIGHT DISAGREEMENT ON THAT LAST POINT

"**OH *YES YOU ARE*, ETHAN** Pitowski," Olivia said later that day, walking home with him and Harley. They walked down a sidewalk interrupted by the bulges of roots from the many trees that lined the streets. They hopped over the crooked concrete. Ethan mostly tried not to trip. "You are *so* going. I'm going. Harley's going. We are all going."

Harley galloped up alongside him, nodding. "It's gonna be *awesome*. It's *Demons of Death* part four, Ethan. Part *four*! I mean, what! I can't even! It's gonna be *so* scary!"

Olivia shot him a look, drawing a thumb across her neck as if to say, *Cool it with the scary talk.*

"Sorry," Harley said. "I mean, it'll probably...not be scary?"

"Yeah right," Ethan said, stooped over from his heavy backpack, his arms crossed in front of him, the flats of his palms tucked under his pits. "You heard what they were saying. People were barfing when they saw it. People died. I don't want to barf or be *near* barf. And I definitely don't want to die."

Harley laughed. "I dunno, sounds kinda rad to me. I mean, not the dying. And not the puking." He paused and said in a lower voice, "Maybe the puking."

Harley already loved horror movies. And weird video games. And heavy metal. His shirt at this very moment had a skull on fire coming out of a dragon's mouth, and inside the *skull's* mouth was some kinda D&D barbarian man playing a guitar that was also a sword. And the sword was on fire. (The band was called Clöd and, according to Harley, was from a place called Swertzendenland, which was not an actual country, but you couldn't convince him of that, and when you tried, he said, "Sorry, I'm not a *geographist*," which also wasn't a thing.)

Olivia danced in front of Ethan, walking backward as he walked forward. "Listen. This is *middle school*, dude. It's shark time. Swim forward or drown. We are *not* the popular kids. We are *not* the cool kids. We do not do sports, are not on student council, are not rich. We are destined to remain sad, lonely weirdos unless—" She made a dramatic flourish of grabbing something out of the air. "*Unless* we seize our destiny. You know how often an invitation like this comes our way? You ever been invited to Kevin Rook's house?" Before either Ethan or Harley could answer, she said: "Yeah, *me either.*"

"Why *are* we being invited?" Ethan asked. "Smells like a trap."

"Everything smells like a trap to you, Ethan." Olivia shrugged. "Think about it. He's inviting the whole dang class because he knows if he doesn't, the kids who *don't* get to go are gonna snitch on his butt. Rook's a jerk, but he's not a stupid jerk."

"I hope he has an indoor pool," Harley said. "And a pool table! Or maybe a pool table that is also a swimming pool somehow. *Or maybe it's all VR.* I totally bet he has VR." Harley stared off into the middle distance. "I bet all of life is a simulation," he whispered to the universe, nodding as if he suddenly understood some deeper truth. Then he ran off to chase a little white butterfly.

Olivia stopped walking, which made Ethan stop too.

"Hey," she said, talking just to Ethan. (Harley was in the middle of the street now. The butterfly was eluding his efforts.) "The movie probably isn't even that scary. Everyone always says this movie or that movie is the scariest thing and then when you watch it, it isn't. You got this. We're a crew, the three of us. The crew has to hang together or it all falls apart. Come with us on Friday night. Please?"

Ethan thought about it.

And the only thought he had about it was *no*.

"I'm good," he said, laughing nervously. "It's fine. It's totally fine. You guys go. I'm not butt hurt about it or anything."

"Ethan."

The way she said it. *Oh no. No no no.*

He tried to hurriedly walk around her, but Olivia darted in his way.

"Aren't you...afraid? Of you not being there? Of missing something cool, some *core memory* of your life happening? Aren't you afraid of people talking about you not being there? Making inside jokes on Monday, jokes we get but you don't, and when you ask about them somebody will be all like, *Oh you wouldn't understand, you weren't at Kevin Rook's awesome house with the swimming pool and the pool table and the virtual reality and the llama rides*—oh, that's right, maybe he has some pet llamas up there on that hill he lives on. You don't know. I don't know. And you can't know until you go. What I'm trying to say is—" And here she leaned in, because she knew she had him. "Aren't you afraid of missing out?"

She knew his weakness.

He was afraid of participating.

But he was afraid of *not* participating.

The same gravity that drew him to the crowd earlier today—

FOMO.

Fear

of

missing

out.

Ahhhhhhhhhhhhhhgggghhh.

But Ethan planted his feet. He shook his head, bearing down like he was in a tug-of-war, and in a way, he was. "No. Nope nope nopeity nope. And—and it's not because I'm scared," he absolutely lied, "it's because I've got tons of homework and my parents won't let me go anyway—and, uh, the only thing I'm scared of is bad grades, and, uh, I don't mean I'm *scared*-scared of bad grades, I just mean I'm *mildly concerned*—no, wait, obviously I'm more concerned than mildly concerned over bad grades because bad grades could derail my entire future—"

"Dude," Olivia said calmly, trying to center him, but it wasn't working this time. He couldn't even get more words out—he was flustered and flummoxed and probably another word that starts with *fl*. So he grunted in frustration (or maybe flustration) and ducked past Olivia, breaking into an awkward run.

"Hey!" she called after him. He knew that tone. He froze.

She walked up to him, poked him dead in the chest, and said three words.

"Humongous. Elephant. Forsythia."

Oh no.

The code phrase.

"I—but—wait," he stammered.

Harley stopped in his butterfly pursuit to echo the three words: "*Humongous elephant forsythia*, man. You heard her."

"I'll—I'll think about it," he told them.

"Ethan, I used the code phrase—"

"Yup okay bye!" he yelled to them, hurrying off.

"Later, dude!" Harley said, waving before once again chasing the butterfly.

"You'll come to Kevin Rook's house!" Olivia hollered. "*Humongous elephant forsythia!*"

SIX
H.E.F.

IT WAS THIRD GRADE WHEN Ethan met Olivia and Harley.

Ethan was getting picked on by a trio of fourth graders and had been for a week. They saw that he was very picky with his eating—he liked to cut his roof-shingle pizza up with a fork and a knife, dicing it into small bits because he was afraid of choking. His mother always told him, "Don't eat so fast. You'll choke," and that had stuck with him like a thorn. He'd sit in the lunchroom with his neatly chopped food and his sketchbook, drawing, every day. But the older kids saw a target, and they went in with mean laughter and cruel eyes. Eventually they started taunting him on the playground by trying to make him eat really gross stuff—dirt the first time, dead leaves the second, a dirty shoelace the third, and by the fourth, a massive earthworm wriggling between pinched fingers. They chased him around mercilessly, threatening to hold him down.

They cornered him on the far side of the playground, by the blue dumpster. As the fourth grader Johnny Hudson closed in on the cowering Ethan, the worm still in hand, Harley came out of nowhere and got right between them. "I'll eat it!" he said, and literally put his open mouth under the worm like he was a seal at an aquarium show—

and slurped it through his lips like a lo mein noodle.
Scchhhhhloooorrrp
Then he cackled.
"More! More! I'm worm hungry!" he said.

The fourth graders gazed at him in horror, not having expected this particular outcome.

That's when Olivia showed up behind them with a bucket.

In that bucket: her homemade unicorn slime. All colors (once a rainbow, but fast turning to a mixed-together mucky brown). Real goopy. Smelled nasty too.

She leapt up and with a swipe managed to splash the backs of all their heads with that foul unicorny goo.

The fourth graders screeched, and pawed at their

heads, which only covered their hands in the rancid slime. They cursed and blubbered and ran away.

Ethan started to hyperventilate, dropping the sketchbook he had been clutching.

"We're all gonna get in so much trouble," he said between gasps.

Olivia picked the sketchbook up, and instantly Ethan's middle tightened and he thought, *Give it back, give it back, oh please, strange girl, give it back.* But instead she kind of held it there, still closed, as she told him, "Nah, it'll be okay. Everybody knows those three are the *woooooorst*, and nobody's going to listen to them unless they suck too."

Olivia and Harley introduced themselves—those two were already friends because they were next-door neighbors, but Olivia added, "But it's really because I'm smart and he's goofy. But we could use a third. You in?"

Ethan didn't know what that meant or why they wanted him, but he nodded. And the rest of recess, they walked around the playground together and talked. Olivia asked to see his sketchbook, and he figured he owed her that much. She didn't say a lot about it, but just gave him a knowing nod and a cool thumbs-up, and that felt like everything to him. At the end of it, when the bell rang, Olivia told him, "I'm gonna watch over you. I'm like Batman and you're Robin. You're my ward."

That's when Harley said, "Awww, I wanna be your word."

"*Ward*, not *word*—"

But Harley didn't listen. "What word can I be? Maybe *elephant*. Or *humongous*. Or *ooh ooh* what's that plant we have in our yard, the one with the yellow flowers? *Forsythia*." He then bellowed all three words together: "HUMONGOUS ELEPHANT FORSYTHIA."

For a while they didn't mean anything much, those three words together, but Olivia had apparently tucked them away in her brain somewhere. One day she was having a real bad day—she didn't do well on a math test, which for Olivia meant a B+, a grade Ethan would have savored on such a test, and Ethan and Harley were making fun of her a little bit for it—not being nice, honestly. Olivia, her jaw set, eyes shining, said those three words again: "Humongous Elephant Forsythia." And they blinked and looked at her like, *Wait, what?* and that's when she said, "Those are our code words. It's our code phrase," she explained, sniffing a little. "When I say them, you know I'm being *real serious*, like I'm real serious right now that you're not being cool to me about this."

They both nodded, because instantly they understood.

(And they apologized to her, as good friends do.)

And that's where it came from, a three-word phrase

useful in all situations, like a linguistic multi-tool. They used the code on one another whenever one of them went too far. It was the kind of saying that might mean something like, *Hey, I need you to do something for me, no fooling.* You know, if they were teasing one another and crossing the line, being too mean, like with that math test? *Humongous Elephant Forsythia*, and they backed off. If they needed one another to lie to a teacher or a parent ("Yes, Mrs. Rickert, it's true that Harley dropped his homework in a pot of French onion soup," which, okay, actually wasn't a lie)? *Humongous Elephant Forsythia.* You needed someone to back you up in an argument, or you needed someone to stand tall against some bullies, or you had low blood sugar and absolutely had to have that Snickers bar in their lunch? *Humongous. Elephant. Forsythia.* And sometimes Ethan could use it on Olivia and Harley when they were getting too wild or about to do something too dangerous—*and* they could use it on him when he was being too shy, too scared, too, well, *too Ethan.*

And this time, that's exactly what Olivia was doing.

Humongous Elephant Forsythia.

Trying to push him out of his comfort zone.

Trying to get them to have fun together.

Trying to keep the crew together.
But going to see that movie...
And using that code phrase against him...
It meant she was serious.
Auuuugh. His stomach hurt just thinking about it.

SEVEN
DEAD LINKS

FOR THE REST OF THE week at Geena Davis Middle School, Kevin Rook's terrifying movie from hell was all anyone could talk about.

In the hall between classes, Ethan was like a lost duckling in rough water pushed this way and that, without room to take off or maneuver. Trapped in this rocking, nauseating current (where he was quite certain he was catching some kind of respiratory illness, because someone around here was coughing like they had a throat full of oatmeal), he caught backpacks to the face, elbows to the neck, even some guy's chin to the top of his head. Finally, he ended up deposited like beach trash into second period social studies, where he heard other kids already talking.

"I hear it's not just the scariest movie ever made, but the goriest."

"Some guy gets chunked by a boat propeller."

"A boat propeller covered in machetes."

"And eels."

"Google said buckets of blood. *Buckets of blood*."

"I hope someone explodes."

"I hope someone gets their eyes popped out by the demon fingers. Or death fingers. Or maybe just the eels. Whatever."

Of course Ethan had done his own quick Googling last night, and in case he needed further confirmation of why he would never want to see this movie, *the internet did provide.* (It always did. Anytime he needed to know if he should be scared of something, Googling it did the trick: Yes, yep, yup, a thousand times yes, be afraid, be very very very afraid. Of everything! All the time!)

And *Demons of Death 4: Death Fingers* was one hundred percent a horror movie to be afraid of.

—◆●◆—

Demons of Death 4: Death Fingers came out in 1991 and showed for one weekend in a half dozen theaters across the Midwest. In that time, it managed to leave a trail of grotesquerie that itself became a kind of legend. Though

Ethan could find no news articles about it, there were plenty of rumors whipping around sites like Florgit and Geekfleek and Cinemaspoon that confirmed exactly the kinds of things the kids in Ethan's class were talking about: barfing and heart attacks among the moviegoers and, on-screen, the aforementioned buckets of blood. People were so upset by the movie that it was swiftly pulled from theaters.

And from there it was like humanity collectively agreed to remove the movie from *reality itself*. It never went to video. Never showed up in video stores, which apparently were a thing once? Even the director, the mysterious Rocky Killdare, disappeared after that—the story being he was so ashamed at his movie's failure that he never made another one again. And the people who made the first three Demons of Death movies claimed they didn't even *approve* the fourth one, saying that it was clearly the work of some deranged fan.

(Though they were glad to capitalize on its legend in even further installments.)

(Which made Ethan wonder if the whole thing was some kind of ruse, a marketing scheme designed to sell other sequels.)

(Ethan was a naturally suspicious kid.)

Supposedly the movie popped up on various video sites

on the dark web now and again, but nobody ever seemed to get to *see* it—by the time they clicked, it was a dead link that led nowhere, the flick already having been removed.

But now, somehow, Kevin Rook seemed to have gotten a copy.

And he was going to show it to the whole sixth grade.

Sixty kids.

Well.

Fifty-nine, anyway.

◆·◆

Olivia was glad to use that number against Ethan at lunch on Wednesday. As Harley wrestled valiantly with a stubborn pudding cup, she told Ethan: "Fifty-nine kids are gonna go to Kevin's house on Friday night, and only one's gonna stay home. You. You're gonna be the weird kid forever."

"Maybe it'll give me some kind of mystique," Ethan said.

"Yeah, mystique like a skunk's butt," Olivia said, frowning.

Harley snorted. "You said 'skunk's butt.' You guys are the best."

Ethan felt queasy.

I'm not gonna go, not gonna go.

But Olivia passed a napkin across the table, and on it was written:

Humongous Elephant Forsythia.

He frowned. She grinned. Harley won the pudding-cup battle and squeezed it into his mouth in one big custardy blob, laughing as he did.

EIGHT
THE TALK

IT WAS FRIDAY.

The day of the movie.

Ethan was not going to go. He wouldn't. Couldn't. It was too scary. He tried to get his friends to do something different, to not go to Kevin Rook's house. Hey, why couldn't they all hang out together, he asked? Olivia said they could. "At Kevin Rook's house," Olivia added, like, *duh*. But Ethan cinched up tight and just couldn't untie the knot inside himself.

He would barely admit that feeling this way made him embarrassed.

Ashamed, honestly.

Because he should be braver than this, he knew.

But he wasn't.

When Ethan was feeling a *certain way* (that is to say, anxious enough that he could crawl the walls like a spider), he did what he always did: He came home from school, closed the door, went to his bed, pulled out his sketchbook from the bowels of his backpack, took out his colored-pencil case from his desk drawer, and then—

Then, Ethan sat down and started to draw.

He never felt afraid while drawing.

It felt like a part of him—a good part, one that he didn't have to worry about. Like the page was a safe space where nobody was judging him. He didn't ever show his work to too many people. Olivia and Harley, obviously: He was always drawing stuff for them, and they always seemed to love it. They never judged him, not like other people would. His art teacher too, Mrs. Saratoga. She always asked to see what he was working on. But everybody else—well, he'd learned they weren't as safe as he wanted them to be. They'd judge him. Or even try to take his sketchbook away. So he mostly kept his drawings to himself. Secret artist and all that.

Today he was finishing a sketch he'd started some weeks ago—another self-portrait (he liked doing those—they made him feel like he was someone else for a while). In this piece, he'd drawn himself as a giant robot, an old-school, old-timey robot with the domed head and bolts everywhere and big stompy metal boots, one of them raised up, ready to crush an unsuspecting city. (Ethan did not want to hurt actual people, so the tiny victims in his drawing were also robots. Tinier, screamier robots.)

It was black and white right now—heavy on the black pencil, almost charcoal. He'd color it in later, maybe.

It was—

Well. It was good.

Ethan knew, somewhere deep, that it was good. Not just this sketch, but most of his work. Mrs. Saratoga always told him he had talent, but that just cinched up his guts further. Because he knew this wasn't something he could do, or should do, or would ever do.

Once upon a time he'd entertained the notion of being a (deep breath) *professional artist*, but that was a silly idea, a foolish notion, an impossible option—

At that, a knock at his door.

He froze.

His blood turned to ice water.

"Ethan?"

A voice through the door.

Dad shouldn't be home yet.

"Uh, okay, hold on—" Ethan said, but it was too late.

Dad was already coming in.

Ethan's father was a soft-bellied balding guy, with big

eyeglasses and tufts of hair on the sides that looked like hurriedly scribbled squiggles of ink. Dad stepped into the room and tensed up when he saw Ethan at the desk. "That homework?" he asked, craning his neck, though he was pretty short, so it was not a successful effort to see past Ethan's splay of arms and hunched shoulders covering his book.

"Yeah, uh, yeah, yes, yup," Ethan said, panicked.

His father walked over to the desk.

Ethan winced.

There were gaps in his coverage. His arms were like twigs—they did not cover up the whole of the drawing. Nor could he hide the colored pencils.

"Oh," his father said, the disappointment in that one word as plain as a booger in a mustache.

"It's not—it's just schoolwork—"

His dad sat on Ethan's bed. "Hey, come sit down."

Ethan sighed. Anxiety twisted inside him like twirling string, tighter and tighter, bundling up until it was no longer thread but an ugly, impossible knot. He stood, then sat next to his father. "It's just a drawing," he tried to say—

Dad interrupted him. "Kiddo, listen. I know. It's nice. It's fun. You—you seem to enjoy it. I just don't want you to get too—"

"Too caught up in it," Ethan said.

"Too caught up in it," his father said at the same time. "Yes, yes, that. I just—you're getting to that age now where you need to start picking a lane. Okay? It's like you're on the highway and if you pick the wrong lane, well, that's the toll lane, and now you're paying a price and you're stuck on that path. You can't just turn around. Next exit might be—who knows?—ten miles down the road. Or maybe you're stuck in this lane and, *oof*, now what? You're on a bridge crossing a river and that bridge is out. You pick that wrong side of the highway and suddenly you're—" Dad flattened his one hand and pushed it off the end of the bed, mimicking what Ethan imagined was a car going over the edge. "Sailing into nothing, into the river." The hand-car went splash into the imaginary water. "And down there in the river is, well, who can say. Rocks, certainly. Fish, probably. Chemicals? I'd think so."

"Dad, I—I don't think highways generally lead to your doom."

"It did for your cousin."

Ethan sighed. "Cousin Julian, I know."

"Cousin Julian, bingo." At that, Dad cupped his hands together and called out for Ethan's mother. "Nance? Nancy! Come on up here!"

"Okie-doke!" she said, her voice drifting up from

downstairs. Ethan did not hear her coming up the steps or down the hall, because his mother was delicate and quiet, like a ninja. She merely appeared at the door, beaming. Mom always beamed. "What's up, Gar-bear?" His father was Gary. *Gar-bear* was her name for him. Gross.

"Tell your son about your sister's kid. Cousin Julian."

"Dad, I know about Cousin Jul—"

But Mom had already started *tsk*ing and shaking her head. "Oh, jeez. Julian, Julian, Julian. Remember what he wanted to be?"

Ethan sighed. *I guess we're doing this.*

"A writer."

"That's right." His mother made a face like she'd just licked the inside of the kitchen trash can. "And how'd that go for him?"

Ethan repeated the story because he'd heard it a hundred times and had to recall it verbally nearly as often. "Now Cousin Julian is thirty years old and he's working at a coffee shop and he doesn't have health insurance and he has to share an apartment with two other weirdos and one of them has an old smelly cat and the other one has six terraria of lizards and—" At this point, all three of them said this last part in unison: "This is Julian's life."

Mom nodded, but then added:

"Just last week he was bitten by a goose."

That was a new wrinkle to the story.

"Chased him down in the park, bit him right in front of a whole gaggle of schoolchildren. Really a shame. Had he made better choices..."

"No goose bite," Ethan said drolly.

Dad nodded, "That's it exactly. No goose bite."

"No goose bite," Mom said. She clucked her tongue again. "Can you imagine: the indignity. And worse, the diseases."

"Goose flu," Dad said.

"All right. Okay. I'm sorry. I'll...put the sketchbook back."

Dad mussed his hair, then frowned at the chaos he'd caused and worked meticulously to put Ethan's hair back in order. "I just want to make sure you're making the best choices, Ethan. That's all. Being an accountant is...well, it's fulfilling work, but stable, always stable. Your mother's job doing logistics for the hospital is steady, good work, good benefits, solid paycheck. This stability feeds the family, keeps us in this nice house, gets us the primo snacks. I just want the best for you and your future. Art is a hard career. It's frivolous. Math, science, engineering: These are the jobs for you. Maybe practice your fractions some more, hmm?"

Sigh.

"Okay, Dad."

"Love you, son."

"Love you too, Dad."

At that, his father stood up. (Though not before arranging one more hair on Ethan's head with a pinch of his thick fingers.) Then he dug into his pockets and pulled out a bottle of hand sanitizer. Ethan knew the deal: He put both of his hands out, Dad spritzed them. A lavender mist burned his nose hairs. Dad sprayed his own hands, then Mom's.

"Okay. Your mother and I are going to grab a bite. It's parent-engagement night. Janine is downstairs. Come say hi to her—and bye to us."

Janine: the babysitter. Nice enough, if completely oblivious to Ethan. But he also didn't give her reason to be involved or invested.

"Be down in a minute," Ethan said.

Dad cast one last forbidding glance at the sketchbook. Ethan knew his father wanted to yoink it from Ethan's grip, and maybe yeet it onto the lawn so it could get hit with the lawn mower. But he didn't. All he said was, "Let's put that away, kiddo."

Then he left the room.

Ethan glumly put his sketchbook back under the bed. And he put his colored pencils away too.

Downstairs he went, to say goodbye to his parents, knowing full well that while they and all the other parents were at the school, their children would be at Kevin Rook's house, watching the scariest stupidest worstest movie ever made.

Well, not him. Ethan was a good kid. He'd stay here. For sure.

NINE
DING

HIS CONVERSATION WITH JANINE, THE babysitter, was the same today as it was every time she came to watch him.

She—eating hyper-sour Japanese candy out of a bag like it was popcorn instead of a mouth-destroying confection probably banned in the United States—sat slumped on the couch, her phone in her hand. Her eyes barely flicked toward him.

"Hey," she said.

"Hey," he said.

"Your mother said your dinner is in the fridge. Gotta microwave it."

"Cool."

"You good, then?"

"I'm good."

And those were the only words they exchanged.

Food in general was an issue for Ethan, because as with everything, competing thoughts chased each other around the racetrack of his mind. Food was good, he had to eat food, but there was the choking thing, and also, what if it gave him food poisoning? Ill-prepared meat and vegetables could definitely give him food poisoning, and the panoply of *beige processed food* (chicken nugs, fish sticks, mac and cheese) that were less likely to poison him were also high in salt. So here he was, worrying about his cholesterol and his sodium intake and (*deep breath*) oh my god was it possible for a twelve-year-old to have a heart attack??

Anyway, Mom had baked a lasagna for tonight.

Mom's food was safe. (After all, she was the one who had taught him about foodborne illnesses and high cholesterol and all that.)

He warmed it up and headed back upstairs, definitely totally not thinking at all about the movie he was too scared to see at the gathering he was too scared to go to. Definitely. Totally. *Agggh.*

Lasagna, eaten. Math, worked on. Mostly. Sort of. Not really? Ethan didn't like math, which was hard because his father *loved* math. Ethan did okay at it, *just* okay, and that maybe broke his father's heart a little. His father was a human calculator. Ethan still occasionally counted on his fingers and toes.

He was still very much *not* thinking about Kevin Rook's theoretical pool, pool table, VR setup, and llama farm. Nope. Not thinking about it at all.

Ethan fidgeted.

It's fine.

They're having fun, but not as much fun as you're having being safe! And not scared! And not throwing up before having a heart attack or whatever! I'm doing math! I'm not getting into trouble! No weird llama diseases here!

Who's winning at life? He numbly pointed at himself. *This guy!*

And then—

His iPad went *ding*.

Ethan did not have a phone (his father wouldn't let him, which was fine, because he did not need phone radiation to explode his brain), but he did have a tablet, because, well, he wasn't Amish. (And don't tell his father, but the drawing apps on the iPad were *pretty cool*.)

He fetched his iPad from the bed—

A fresh text from Olivia:

> HUMONGOUS. ELEPHANT. FORSYTHIA. 🚨🚨🚨

Followed by a bunch of siren emojis.

Ethan shrank.

He feared missing out, obviously, but here was Olivia, again invoking their code. And here he was, not swayed by it. That was a betrayal, wasn't it? Of her? Of Harley?

Oh, ohhh no.

What if they stopped being friends with him over this? What if he was in fact (*gasp*) *breaking up the crew*? What if they came out of the party with a *new crew*? Some other third person who was not Ethan Pitowski? Maybe there was a cool kid from another school, and now that kid was their best friend? Or a kid kind of like Ethan, who kept them from doing anything too crazy, but yet who was fun and *not* scared all the time and somehow actually *liked* scary movies?

Ethan wanted to scream.

Just then, another message came in. A video.

Don't play it.
Don't play it.
You know you shouldn't pl—
But he was already playing it.

And there was Olivia, standing in a massive finished basement lit dimly with a kind of cool purply party glow. A huge crowd of kids hung around. On the far wall, someone had set up what looked like an old-as-eternity TV—heavy as a tank and shaped like a hay bale. Right now it showed a blue screen. A smaller device sat atop it—*the VCR?* Ethan wondered. He'd never seen one in person.

Nor will you, because you're not going to that party, he reminded himself.

Olivia thrust her face right up into the camera.

"Dude. You're not here. You need to *be* here. Movie starts at seven p.m., which is in thirty minutes, and you need to *get here*."

Suddenly, the camera jostled and the microphone did that thing where it was like *pssh shmmpff fwwp* because someone was putting their hands over it, and now Olivia's face was joined by Harley's, his mouth ringed with what was likely a volcanic crust of dust from Flamin' Hot Cheetos.

"ETHAN OMG LOOK," and again the camera jostled, and this time it spun wildly, faces melting as it whirled around, until it finally stopped and settled on some kind of table. Two kids were there, one standing at each end. Harley's head again filled the screen, eyes wide. "It's better than a pool table," he said rapturously. "It's air hockey. AIR HOCKEY, ETHAN. And I've had so many Mountain Sweat Ultra Nuclear Swamp Coolers that I can *see through space and time* to a place beyond humanity where the Star People wait to teach us their ways and—" He burped suddenly, a thunderous gastric tumble.

Olivia reappeared, wresting the phone away from Harley.

"Ethan. *Ethan*. People are wondering where you are. People like—"

And there appeared Kevin Rook.

Slick, cool rich kid Kevin Rook.

He winked at the camera. "Owen. Hey, man, where are you?"

"*Ethan*," Olivia whispered to him.

"*Pfah*, whatever. Get down here, it's rad, no cap. It's real sus you're not here, bro. Everybody's here, Steven. Everybody"—Kevin brought the camera right up to his face—"*except you*."

And then the message ended.

Ethan's heart was racing. His palms were sweaty

even as his mouth felt weirdly dry. His mind was a Jenga tower, wobbling. He was afraid to pluck at any one piece of it, lest the whole thing fall.

Kevin Rook told me to come.

Or Owen or Steven or whatever he thought Ethan's name was.

Still.

He'd asked for *him*.

All the other kids were there.

Ethan paced. Anxieties chased him, nipping at his heels like bitey Chihuahuas. *Too many kids. A scary movie—the scariest movie, in fact, of all time. I don't belong. I'm gonna do something embarrassing. My pants will fall down. I'll fall down. I'll cry at the movie. I'll scream like a scared rabbit. Better to stay here. It's cooler to not go. I'm cool. I'm totally cool.*

He was not cool.

He wasn't feeling cool. Nobody thought he was cool.

Agh agh agh agh.

He looked at the time. Already ten minutes had passed somehow since he'd watched the message.

His iPad dinged again.

Olivia. No video. Just a text.

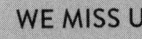

Then another:

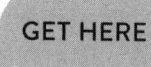

Ethan bit down on his own teeth so hard he thought they'd turn to powder.

His internal scream became an external one—small, contained, repressed, but external just the same. *"Ahhhhhhhhh."*

And at that, he hurried downstairs, overwhelmed by the sudden feeling of being in a car driving off a bridge into the chasm below.

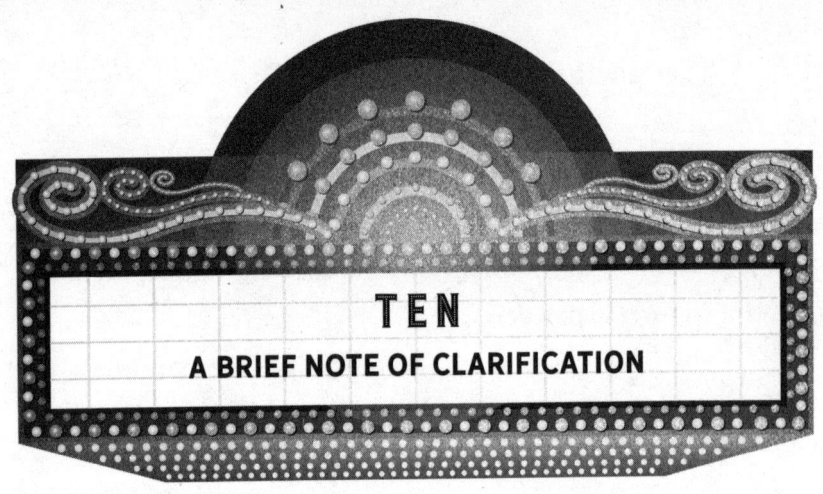

TEN
A BRIEF NOTE OF CLARIFICATION

NOT THAT ETHAN WOULD EVER be near an actual waterfall. Or a boat. Oh, gosh, he'd never go on a boat. A boat was on water, and water wanted to drown you, and also there were *things* inside water, like biting eels. Oh no, did he have a thing about eels now? A fixation? A compulsive, intrusive thought? Were there eels in him right *now*? No, no, of course there weren't. That was silly.

Unless there were.

Aaaaaaaah.

Inside his mind, he heard Olivia's voice:

Dude, you're spiraling.

And he was. He knew it. He could feel it.

Deep breaths.

In, out.

In, out.

You trust your friends, he told himself.

WE MISS U, she had texted.

And that was when he knew what was going to happen next.

ELEVEN
DOWN AND OUT

AS HE PASSED JANINE ON the couch, he said, "I'll, uhhhh, be right back."

"Cool," she said, not looking up from her phone, the candy rattling hard against her teeth.

Out the door Ethan went.

I'll be right back. It wasn't a lie. It was his brand-new plan. He'd go! He'd go *and* he'd only stay for, like, a couple of minutes. Ethan would be there long enough for everyone to *see* he was there, for his friends to stop feeling like he was breaking up the crew, and then the movie would start, and then quietly, like a cool, anxious ninja, he'd duck out the back. Then he'd bike back home, and his parents would never know he'd been gone.

Easy-peasy, Charmin squeezy.

Kevin Rook did not live in their neighborhood. Their neighborhood was what Ethan's father called "middle class," though Ethan had only a peripheral understanding of what that meant. He did know, however, that Kevin Rook was rich. Because Kevin Rook would tell you himself: "I'm mega rich." He said his father was a billionaire, but Ethan's dad said that he was most certainly not a billionaire, probably just a millionaire. The kind of person who could buy a really fancy car, but not, say, their own villainous island.

Still, that meant Kevin Rook lived two neighborhoods over.

Past Fox Lake was Emerald Glen, where the houses got nicer, the yards got bigger. Past Emerald Glen was Pastoral Farms, which had very few farms but a lot of wide-open space just the same: It was barely a neighborhood at all, mostly a stretch of farmhouses revamped to look semi-modern, plus a scattering of something called McMansions, which Ethan assumed was the fast-food equivalent of a mansion? Didn't matter.

Point was, Kevin Rook's house was almost perfectly in the center of town. It sat up on a hill, looking down on everyone else, Kevin and his parents living like suburban royals.

(Them and, if Olivia had it right, llamas.)

(Though Ethan figured the llamas were wishful thinking.)

(He *hoped* they were wishful thinking because, y'know. Llama diseases.)

Kevin Rook's house in the center of town was about a twenty-minute bike ride away.

Or, it would've been.

Just as Ethan was approaching the hill leading up to the big sprawly Rook house, all modern and ugly and blocky, he felt a faint *thump-a-bump* as his bike rode over something. Then he heard a hiss—moments before the tire started to go *fa-thwup fa-thwup fa-thwup*. Ethan nearly fell off the bike, which only confirmed his greatest fears about riding a bike in the first place. He almost never rode anywhere, because of exactly this problem—and when he did, like now, he wore a helmet, and elbow guards, and shin guards, *just in case*. (Olivia said it made him look like a dork. But his answer was, "Yes, a dork whose body is not a gravel-crusted rag doll on the highway." To which she said, "Still a dork, though," and then she punched him in the arm and laughed, and he laughed too because, well, he didn't know why.)

Ethan got down under the bike—

And saw a nail sticking in the rubber. Air gassing out around it.

"No no no," he muttered from between clenched teeth.

With the bike's front tire shrinking like his confidence, he realized a new horror: *My parents are going to know.* They'd see the ruined tire. They'd know he went out. And worse, he was going to have to get home with the ruined bike, walking it all the way, which would double the time of his trip.

He was *so* close.

The house was

Right

up

there.

He could see it.

He could almost smell Harley's battery-acid Mountain Sweat soda breath. He could practically feel Olivia hugging him before slugging him in the arm.

Darkness was setting in now.

I'm not going to cry.

He blinked back tears burning at the edges of his eyes. He felt helpless and trapped. *I should go home. No. I should go to the party. No. I should go home. Party.*

Home. Party. Home. But all Ethan managed to do was stand there, shaking, holding his bike with the busted front tire.

And that's when he heard it, echoing out over the growing dark:

A scream.

TWELVE
THE SCREAM

IT... *WAS* A SCREAM, RIGHT? It was muffled. Like it came from inside the house. It even sounded a *little* bit like...

Olivia.

Well, it made sense people were screaming in there. They were watching a horror movie after all. The scariest one ever made. Of course there was screaming. Probably some yarfing. Maybe even a heart attack or two.

But...

What if something was wrong?

What if it *was* Olivia?

What if she was in trouble? Or worse, *in danger*?

He heard her voice again inside his head:

You're spiraling, dude.

She was fine. Everyone was fine. Scary movies made people scream.

Still.

Olivia was his friend. His best friend.

Okay, Harley was also his best friend—they were both his best friends—and he refused to believe in the kind of limited thinking that demanded a person have only one best friend.

He had to check on her. Had to. It was the thing a best friend did. Ethan would just go up to the house, see what was up. Besides, he had already committed to going in there like his friends had asked him to. Humongous Elephant Forsythia.

He looked down at the bike. *You stay here*, he told it, as if it were a loyal horse and not a busted bicycle.

Then he took a deep breath and ascended the hill toward Kevin Rook's house. Everything would be fine, he knew. That couldn't have been a real scream.

Could it?

The pathway to the front door of Rook's big sprawly house was a winding one through all manner of meticulously planted flowers and modernist sculptures. It was lit up—unlike the house itself, which Ethan realized was weirdly dark.

No, it's not weird, he told himself. That was normal.

The kids were in the basement, right? And the parents were at the school, for parent-engagement night. Of course the place would be dark instead of lit up like a stadium.

Still. His hands were sweaty again. His mouth drier than the stuff inside a vacuum bag. He rang the doorbell, trying not to jump out of his own skin.

The sound of the doorbell was not the classic *ding-dong* but, rather, an electronic-sounding *bonnnng*.

No one came to the door.

Ethan did a pee-pee dance even though he didn't actually have to go. It was just nerves. He hesitated, then poked the doorbell again.

And still nothing.

Okay that's weird, right?

No, it wasn't weird, he told himself.

But it feels weird.

He explained to his own brain, *No, it's probably loud down in the basement.* They can't hear you.

Go home.

Get your bike.

Go home.

But—

He remembered the scream.

Olivia's scream.

It wasn't Olivia.

Couldn't have been. And yet, the only way to really confirm that, *because he didn't have a phone*, was to go inside and see her. She'd be there. She'd be proud of him for coming. She'd be not screaming at all. Then he'd say he had to go to the bathroom and quickly run away, hopefully dragging his bicycle home before his parents got there and—then what? He couldn't worry about that now.

Ethan tried the door.

It was unlocked.

It opened into a dark, quiet house.

Go home go home go home go home.

He sucked in a breath, held it deep—

And went inside.

THIRTEEN
THE BLUE GLOW IN THE BASEMENT

IT OCCURRED TO HIM TOO late: This was not his house. He was breaking in, sorta. Did they have security? Cameras? Would they call the police on him? Would he go to jail, oh god? He had to remind himself: *You're supposed to be here. You were invited, you goof. Kevin Rook was on video asking you to come.* Still. This not being his house meant he had no idea where anything, or anyone, was. And it was big.

So through the darkness he crept, through a foyer that was bigger than his living room, through a living room that was bigger than his whole house, into a kitchen that probably could've had an entire kitchen staff. He tried to stay quiet, but his shoes clicked and tapped across marble floors, then across hand-sculpted hardwoods that also added a few creaks and squeals.

He tried one door—

Just a trash-can closet. A whole closet for a trash can. A big trash can. *They must have a lot of trash*, he thought. Idly, he wondered if he could just climb into the trash and hide there forever, like Oscar the Grouch. Except he'd probably catch some sort of trash-based infection in there.

He closed the door.

A breeze ruffled his hair. He saw then that there was an open sliding door leading to the back patio. But there weren't many lights on and nobody seemed to be out there. It was just...open.

He hurried over and slid it shut with a click. Just, you know. In case. In case of monsters. Which weren't real. Obviously. Ha ha. Ha.

Ethan turned back toward the kitchen.

It was so quiet in the house that the silence seemed to be its own noise. Shouldn't he be hearing the movie? Or kids freaking out? Screaming and laughing? Or maybe crying and puking? Shouldn't he hear the distant sound of an ambulance as it came to rescue all the kids whose hearts were exploding under the onslaught of the Scariest Movie Ever Made?

He listened harder. Maybe they just had really good sound dampening down in the basement....

And that's when he heard it—

White noise punctuated by a pulsing, throbbing sound.

...Vwom...

...Vwom...

...Vwom...

Like a staticky heartbeat.

It was coming from beneath him.

He crossed the broad kitchen and found another door, which opened to a set of steps. Carpeted steps to a finished basement? Seemed like.

A blue glow, flickering like firelight, greeted him—almost like neon floodwater rising up from below.

The thrumming sound grew louder with the doorway open.

VWOM. VWOM. VWOM.

No sounds from a movie. No sounds from kids.

Just the blue glow and the pulsing hum.

Ethan gingerly took a step down even as every cell in every muscle in his body tried to revolt and send him screaming in the other direction.

Olivia.

Harley.

He had to know they were okay.

So he forced himself to take another step. And another. And onward until he was at the bottom, which opened up into an expansive basement—the very same one he'd seen on Olivia's video. It was bathed in the blue glow here—a glow emanating from the huge old-school TV against the wall. And it was from the speakers on the TV that the humming thrum seemed to come—

VWOM VWOM VWOM

Thing was:

The kids were all here.

They were sitting on couches. On chairs. Some on the floor. Others stood against the far wall. And all of them stared dead ahead, perfectly still. Their mouths hung open. And their eyes glowed a flickering, pulsing blue.

At first Ethan thought it was just the reflection from the TV, but—no, their eyes were glowing.

Dead and bright.

None of them turned toward him as he entered the basement. They didn't budge or flinch.

"Guys," he said in a small voice.

Nothing. No movement. No recognition that he was here.

VWOM VWOM VWOM

They're staring at the TV, he realized.

"Guys?" he said, louder this time.

Still nothing.

He scanned the faces through the blue light—Harley was against the back wall. "Harley," Ethan hiss-whispered toward him. Then: "Olivia?" he asked, looking around.

She wasn't here.

Okay, that's weird.

And then—

VWOMVWOMVWOM

Was that sound pulsing faster? Like an excited heartbeat. Ethan thought it was. Up in pitch, too.

Shaking now, he hurried quickly past a corner bar top loaded with snacks and drinks, around the air hockey table, toward Harley.

Harley had a movie-theater bag of popcorn in his hand, except it was dangling upside down—a little hill of popcorn sat at his feet. His jaw was slack. His tongue sat on his lower lip like a slug sunning itself on a rock.

He was breathing.

But he wasn't blinking.

Ethan couldn't even *see* his eyeballs. Harley's whole eye was just blue, like the screen on the TV.

Ethan poked him.

"Harley!"

Nothing.

He gave him a light push. Harley's head went *dunk* against the wall, and more popcorn fell out of his bag.

But still, no reaction at all.

Ethan was about to say Harley's name again when there was a sharp *crack* from the other side of the room. Ethan startled—and he was the only one who did. He whipped around to look.

The big, chunky TV shuddered in place—

And when it did, the air split again with a loud *cra-crack!*

Ethan flattened against the wall next to Harley.

That's when the TV started to move.

FOURTEEN
THE MONSTER MOVIE

THE TV ROSE UP OFF its stand, into the air, carried on a column of darkness. The blue glow flickered. The sound quickened as the TV rose higher. *VWOMVWOMVWOM-VWOM*. Until it stopped suddenly with another *cra-crack!*

The pillar of darkness beneath the TV split in two.

Into—

Legs, Ethan realized.

Long, spindly legs. Darker than night. Like they were rips in the paper of the universe. Then the TV shuddered again, more violently this time—

Crrrraaaack!

And two more limbs emerged from the television, one on each side—

Arms. But insectile, with many joints, bent in too

many places and in odd directions. The end of each dark arm bloomed like a shadowy flower, and a dozen fingers on each end tickled the air.

The TV wobbled and pushed up, up, up, popping out over the spindly limbs onto a neck. It had legs, it had arms, and now—

The television was its head.

The blue glow on the screen flickered one last time—

And then went dark.

Ethan clamped his hands over his own mouth to suppress a scream.

The room was plunged into pure shadow. It stunned his eyes, left him searching for something, for anything he could see—

His gaze found purchase once more, and there he saw it: a shape darker than the darkness around them, still against the opposing wall. The TV-headed thing rose tall, stooping so that it did not bump its head into the low ceiling—

The screen flicked on once more.

But now, the blue glow was gone.

In its place:

A single eyeball with a snowstorm of black-and-white static at its center.

It hissed with the static sound: *kkkksshshhhhhhhh*.

It spun its eyeball toward him—

Ethan bit back a fearful squeak and dropped to the floor, next to Harley and behind the long sectional couch on which sat many of his classmates.

The static glow from the eyeball and the hissing white noise of the creature became his only way to track the thing's movements: It began to roam to the left side of the room, around the far edge of that couch, toward where some other kids were sitting in beanbags and video-game chairs. It stalked silently, making no footfalls. It stopped moving for a moment, the glow dimming just a little—

It's looking away from me, he thought.

I should run.

I should hide.

I should stay and help my friends.

I should go home.

Panic bored through him like chewing ants. He felt like he was going to cry. He felt like he was going to pee. He wanted to scream. He wanted to shrink into nothing. He wanted this to be over, please, please, *please*.

Worst of all? Ethan had no idea what to do.

His mind was a carousel of options spinning faster and faster.

Before he did anything—

He knew he had to look.

Had to *see*.

So he gripped the top edge of the couch and lifted himself up just to the level of his nose, so that he was peering over the cushions between the heads of who he thought might be Rachel Malinenko and Bart Wallace—

Screenhead stood in the far corner, its ink-dark back bent in a crooked stoop, its spine ridged with black spires. It dipped its eyeball-screen head toward Teddy Woodhull, who sat slumped back in a beanbag chair, a soda can trapped in the soft grip of his slackened hand against his chest, a stain of it slowly spreading across his shirt. Screenhead fixed its one eye upon the boy, almost inquisitively, as if it were scrutinizing him, looking for something, *considering* something. Teddy didn't react at all, just remained there, staring dead ahead at the space where the television once sat. Screenhead leaned forward.

That's when the image on its screen-face changed.

The eye flickered into a spray of static.

And it was replaced by a mouth.

A mouth of twisted lip and yellow teeth.

Ethan watched, rapt in horror, as the screen slowly descended onto the top of Teddy's head, and it was like—well, it was like that screen was just made of water, because Teddy's head sank into it without a sound. The screen glowed extra white where it touched Teddy's face and head—over his forehead, now his ears, now down past his nose and mouth—

All the while, Ethan wanted to scream out, wanted to warn Teddy, wanted to run away himself and pretend none of this was happening—it was just a dream, a nightmare given life. Maybe he fell off his bike and knocked his own skull for a loop and this was the vision he was having after plunging into unconsciousness.

But it felt real.

All too real.

Now Teddy's head was all the way gone—like it was in the mouth of a lion, except in this case the lion was a glowing TV with a bent, somehow-bony, somehow-also-liquid dark body.

If it kept stooping down, bending over farther, the TV would swallow Teddy whole.

But it didn't keep going. It stopped there, past his head, at the neck.

Then—

It made a new sound. Like a wet *chomp*. The sound of someone eating a juicy, crisp apple with great gusto.

Screenhead stood back up as straight as it could.

As for Teddy, well—

Teddy's head was *gone*.

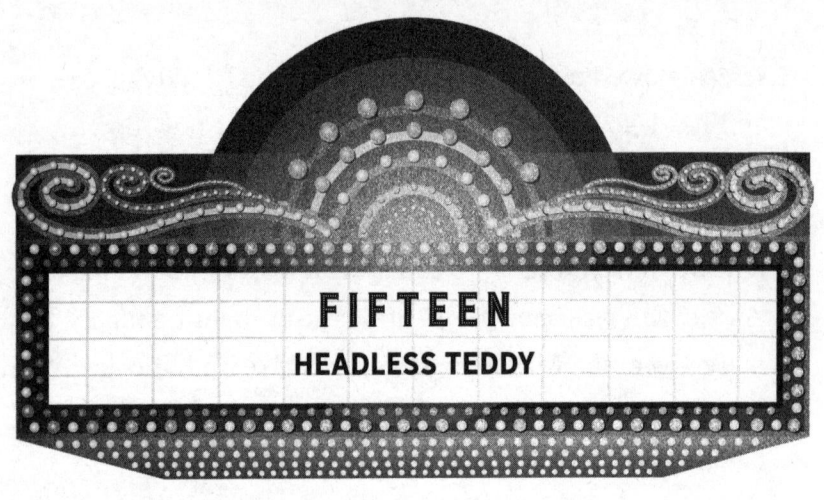

FIFTEEN
HEADLESS TEDDY

WITH THE TAKING OF TEDDY'S head, there was no blood, no mess, no muss, no fuss—as Screenhead's screen-face flickered back to an eye as if to regard its work, Ethan saw that Teddy's head was simply gone, as if it had never existed at all. It was like a doll whose head had been popped off, end of story.

Ethan, of course, wanted very badly to scream.

To scream and scream and scream some more.

And that desire to scream only increased as he watched Screenhead stalk to the next sixth grader—Billy Senf, sitting in one of the video-game chairs—before turning its screen back to the yellow-teethed mouth and stooping more swiftly this time to dunk Billy's whole head into the liquid screen of the monster's sort-of-face.

The screen flickered. Ethan watched the teeth glitch, then close. And then came a wet celery-ripping sound—

Billy Senf's head was gone now too. The spot where his head had been was now just a patch of smooth skin, no eruption, no disruption, no nothing.

Screenhead stalked to the next kid.

Ethan sank back down behind the couch. He tried to cover his ears, but he still felt the vibrations of the monster's footfalls, still heard the intrusive sound of the apple-bite, yellow-toothed beheadings happening—*chomp, chormp, schlomp.*

One by one it walked.

From kid to kid.

And soon it would circle around the couch.

To where Ethan was.

And to Harley.

Harley!

He grabbed his friend's leg by the ankle and shook it like he was a toddler trying to get a parent's attention. Nothing.

He hated to do it, but he balled his hand into a fist and slugged Harley in the shin. Then the knee. Still Harley stared ahead, his eyes shining with only the flickering blue light of a dead TV screen.

C'mon c'mon c'mon!

The footsteps came closer. The shadows around Ethan darkened as the glow from Screenhead's facescreen shined brighter. *It's almost here.*

One last-ditch effort, then.

Harley was wearing shorts—he pretty much always wore shorts, even in winter. Cargo shorts stuffed with all manner of junk, from half-melted chocolate to D&D figurines to guitar picks. One time he found a forgotten ham sandwich in a pocket. He didn't know how long it had been there. He ate it anyway. So, now, with his calf exposed—

Ethan took a deep breath, opened his mouth, and bit down on Harley's leg.

Not hard enough to draw blood.

But sure as anything to leave a bruise.

And at that, Harley flinched, crying out as his knee popped up reflexively—

Right into Ethan's face. Fireworks burst behind his eyelids as he toppled backward, his nose throbbing and eyes watering. He blinked through his tears and saw the bleary, greasy shape of the monster suddenly slinking over the top of the couch, effortlessly, silently, *frictionlessly*, like some kind of spider monkey made of liquid shadow: Its screen flashed white and blue. From the eye to the mouth. It moved fast, descending upon Harley.

Harley swatted at it, crying out. But he was too slow. The monster darted in faster than Ethan had seen it move before—

Its screen a hungry mouth.

And Harley's head an enticing target.

SIXTEEN
THAT FAMILIAR FROZEN FEAR

ETHAN BACKPEDALED AWAY FROM THE creature as it moved toward Harley. His mind was like a rat on a rapidly sinking ship, scrambling for an exit, unsure where to go or what to do or how to escape the vessel plunging into the rising waters. He wanted to save Harley, but how? Cry out? Throw something? Throw what? Jump up? Punch the monster and lose his own head? Did he even know how to punch anything except in a video game? He was too scared to make any decision at all—the paralysis of panic was real. He was afraid for Harley and for himself, so all he could do was cower there on the floor, trembling, as the creature bent forward—

No no no no no!

The glitching TV-screen mouth closing in—

Ethan shut his eyes so hard, he thought he was going to pass out.

But he did not close his ears, and that's when he heard it—

Chrommmp

Ethan's eyes popped open.

It had taken Harley's head.

Harley's body slumped backward against the wall, still standing, but now without the mulleted head that, well, made him so very Harley.

Panic was the only choice Ethan had now, and his body seized and freaked out—the rat in his brain was running things now, taking over his body like the soup-making rodent in that Pixar movie, and he quickly kicked out at the carpeted floor, gaining clumsy purchase with his feet before launching himself back around the other side of the couch—

Just in time for the staticky glow of Screenhead's searching eye to find the space where Ethan had been seconds before.

Seeing a coffee table in front of the couch, Ethan pulled himself underneath it, for he was a fairly small kid who could, when called to do it, zip himself up in a suitcase as a stunt. (Well, okay, he had never actually zipped himself into a suitcase. He was zipped *into* a suitcase by his cousin Marnie. Julian's little sister. She'd shoved him in there and closed it up, and there Ethan had waited, sure he was going to die trapped in an airless suitcase or, stranger still, that he'd accidentally end up on a plane and the plane would take him to a faraway destination where he didn't speak the language and didn't know anybody and he'd never see his friends or family ever again.)

From under the table, he peered out.

He saw the kids who were sitting on the couch, now without their heads. No faces, no eyes, no ears or cheeks or chins or hair. Just open air as they sat there, snacks and drinks in their laps. And behind them, Screenhead stalked the basement, going from kid to kid to kid. Chomping away.

Ethan bit down on his own hand so he didn't screech, squeal, or scream.

Because he knew if he did—

It would come for him, too.

All the while, the scrambling rat in his brain clung to a single piece of driftwood in the ocean of nightmare he was experiencing:

Olivia was not here.

Her scream maybe meant she'd escaped.

On the one hand, he was glad she wasn't here.

On the other hand...he really, really wished she were

with him right now. Because Olivia always knew what to do. She was bold and brave and wasn't ever trapped by her fear or her indecision. She'd probably kick this thing in the face and then watch Netflix on its creepy head somehow. But all Ethan could do was hide and cower and try very hard not to make sad, scared noises—even as the spidery-limbed shadow-bodied TV-headed monster silently stalked around the room, seeking just one more head to eat with its horrible, glitching mouth.

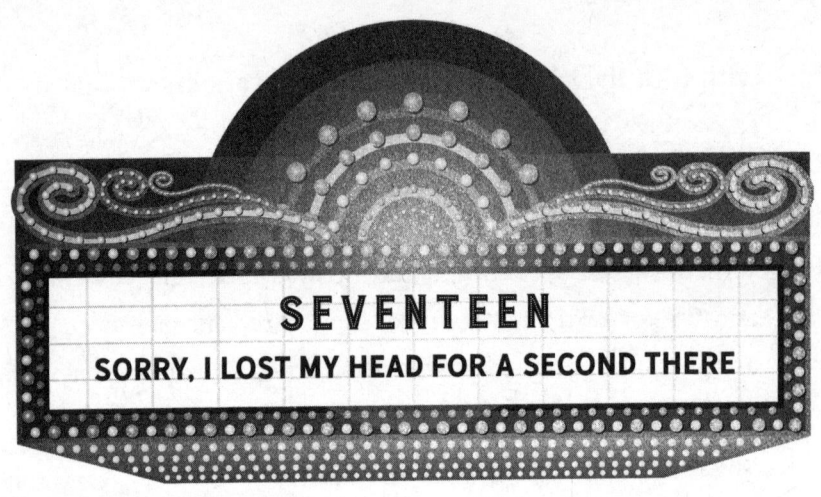

SEVENTEEN
SORRY, I LOST MY HEAD FOR A SECOND THERE

ONCE UPON A TIME, ETHAN did fly on an airplane. He'd taken a trip from here in Pennsylvania to Boston for the third (or maybe fourth) wedding of his Aunt Meredith, who was, in his father's words, "a marriage Houdini," whatever that meant. The flight was less than two hours, and during that time, Ethan sat in his chair, quaking in near-constant fear as they passed through a pocket of rough air that bounced the plane around so badly, his teeth were clacking.

His father and mother both were white-knuckling the armrests. Ethan sat in the aisle seat, his entire emotional landscape a tornado of anxiety. He wanted to throw up. They were going to die.

But then, across the aisle from him sat a guy chewing

gum, messy hair almost in his eyes. He looked over and winked and said, "Nervous flier?"

Ethan nodded a little.

"Hey," the guy said, "don't sweat it. I was too, once. But look at it this way: The plane wants to stay up in the air, it's how they're designed. The turbulence is just like bumps on the road. Soon the road will smooth out and the turbulence will be over."

"How do you know?" Ethan asked.

The guy shrugged and laughed. "I'm an aerospace engineer. I design planes."

"Oh."

Another wink and the guy went back to chewing gum and reading a book he had sitting in his lap.

At the moment, Ethan had thought darkly, *Sure, stranger, the turbulence will be over when we crash*, but the guy was right. The so-called road up in the air did in fact smooth out. The turbulence softened, then ended.

Hiding under the coffee table now felt kind of like that, like the Screenhead creature would carry on its horrid head harvest forever, that it would go around and around the room until finally it found him and his juicy, delicious head. (Assuming, of course, the monster ate heads because they were tasty and not for some more obscure purpose.) But eventually—

It stopped.

It stood there for a moment, its boxy head turning this way and that, as if it were listening, or working to sense vibrations in the air.

Ethan held his breath.

Felt his heartbeat in his cheeks, his neck, his ears. *Wub wub. Wub wub.*

And then, just like that—

The creature slinked away like some kind of arachnid cheetah, dropping to all fours and disappearing up the steps in total silence.

Ethan knew not to move.

Not to speak.

To only barely *breathe*.

Because, though he didn't watch horror movies, not at all, not ever, he knew from Google what would happen next. Come out of hiding too early, what happened? The monster heard you and came back to getcha. *Chomp chomp.*

So he waited for a long time. How long? He didn't know, because he wouldn't even hazard a glance at his watch in case the glow resummoned the creature.

Finally, though, his body cramping, his heart rate dropping from *horse galloping across a field on fire* to *terrified pony walking in circles,* Ethan knew it was time to get up and figure out what to do next.

He crawled out from under the table.

He looked around the room. It was mostly dark now, with the creature's glow gone. Both the TV and VCR on the back wall were truly gone, having transformed together into *that thing.* Ethan's eyes adjusted enough that he could see what he was doing—so he walked over to a nearby standing lamp and clicked it on.

Blinking past the white glow, he took a fresh gander around and again felt horror sinking into him like a deep stain.

All these kids. His classmates. He wasn't close with most of them. More than a few were mean, but a lot of them were nice enough, cool enough. Rachel Malinenko always called him "a weird egg," so okay. Hunter Coogins was always joking, even though it got him into trouble. Bart Wallace was hecka smart, Casey Dawson was a great artist, and Teddy was, like, a video game *maestro.* But still, to see them like this. And Harley…

Sweet, human golden retriever Harley.

They were all—

Headless.

Which meant—

Dead, right? They were dead. They had to be dead.

Except—

Ethan flinched, and peered closer.

His eyes scanned each of them, going from one to the next.

They were breathing.

Somehow. Some way. It felt beyond impossible because, uh, where were they breathing from? They didn't have mouths or noses or even, *ew*, neck holes or anything. There were just smooth Silly Putty skin patches where their heads had been, and yet, just the same—they were breathing. They were drawing breath into their bodies.

Ethan hurried around to Harley—

He pressed an ear to his friend's chest, and it was super creepy because, again, *Harley had no head*, but what did Ethan hear?

A heartbeat.

Harley was *alive*.

They all were.

That meant—

Well, that meant they could get their heads back. Right? Conceivably? Maybe? Ethan didn't really understand how, or what any of this even meant. It seemed entirely beyond the realm of possibility, but then again, so did a TV growing arms and legs and a body and traipsing around a finished basement, disappearing heads and leaving the headless bodies alive.

None of this made sense.

But if Ethan could figure it out—if he *could* make sense of it?

Maybe he could save his friend, and his classmates, too.

First he had to find Olivia.

He did one last scan of the kids to make sure she wasn't here—

And she wasn't.

But then he noticed something strange.

Olivia wasn't the only one who was missing.

Where the heck was Kevin Rook?

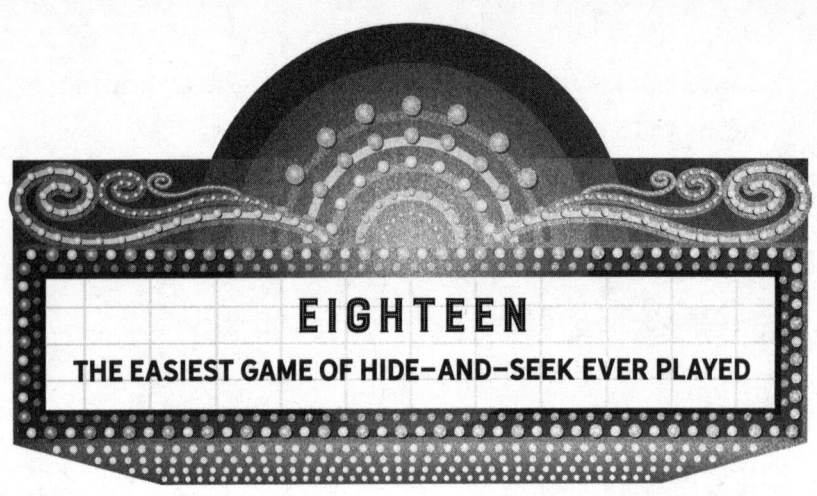

EIGHTEEN
THE EASIEST GAME OF HIDE-AND-SEEK EVER PLAYED

TURNING ON THE LAMP HAD revealed a pair of doors at the far side of the basement. One door said HVAC on a little shiny plaque. The other door said WASHROOM, which, Ethan supposed, was a fancy person's way of saying, *Here is where the toilet lives.*

Ethan's hand paused over the doorknob for the washroom.

A tremor of new fear crawled through him.

What could be on the other side of the door?

Another headless child? Another monster? A pit of spikes and darkness, bottomless, full of eels, probably? (It occurred to Ethan only now that he was perhaps overly worried about eels in his life. Which itself was a new worry—the worry about being worried. Ethan's mind was a circus of anxiety.)

He shut down the train of terrible thoughts going through his head.

I gotta do it, he knew. What if Olivia was inside and needed help?

Ethan threw open the door.

And there sat Kevin Rook.

He was hugging the toilet the way someone with a stomach bug does. Ethan had a stomach bug so bad one time, he basically slept on the bathroom floor all night. It had been coming out of him at each end. Ethan had been convinced that he was dying, or maybe already dead.

But Kevin Rook didn't look sick.

He looked—

Well, *scared*.

He had been crying. That much was clear. His eyes were puffy and red. His nose, goopy with frothed snot. Kevin blinked when he saw Ethan.

"Wh...what happened?"

Ethan looked behind him, then back to Kevin. "You don't know?"

Kevin shook his head and stood up.

"You're Steven, right?"

Eye roll.

"Ethan," Ethan said, rather Ethanly. *We're in the same class, Kevin, jeez.*

"Oh. Oh yeah." Ethan stepped aside, letting Kevin step into his own basement and see what had happened while he hid.

Kevin started to stammer: "I—I—so I put, like, the movie on and—and then this warning came up, but it was, like, handwritten or something, and everybody started to watch, like *really* watch, and I knew it was gonna be hella scary so I—I went to the bathroom, but then I heard these...these *noises* and I peeked out and—"

But his words dried up in his mouth, grapes to raisins. All that came out now was a creaking noise, like floorboards under a pressing foot, because he was seeing—like, *really* seeing—all his headless classmates.

"Oh, oh god, *oh god.*"

He flattened himself against the back wall, until he realized he was standing only feet from headless Harley.

At that, Kevin Rook *screamed.*

A high-pitched, glass-cracking scream that went on and on and on. Ethan had to clamp his hand over Kevin's mouth. "Shh! *Shh.* Or it'll come back!"

Kevin blinked.

"It?"

"Yes. It."

"Right. Right. I—I saw it, just for a second. What the heck was it?"

"It's an...an *it*, a *thing*, a *monster*."

Kevin was still clearly not getting it, so Ethan explained.

"I don't know what it was, okay? The TV was just sitting there, and then it sprouted arms and legs and a body and a neck and...everybody was just, like, *staring* at it." *Hypnotized*, he realized. Like how that snake hypnotized the kid in *The Jungle Book*. "It crept around the room, its screen-face becoming a mouth before...before biting their heads off."

It took a few moments before Kevin started screaming again, and before Ethan had to once more slap his hand over the other boy's mouth.

"Please! It'll come back for us! Please stop screaming!"

Slowly, Kevin nodded.

Ethan unclamped his hand.

"I didn't know this would happen," Kevin said in a small voice.

"I figured that."

"I just wanted to mess with everyone, that's all."

Pause.

Blink, blink.

"Wait, what?"

"I—they said it was the scariest movie ever, and I wanted everyone to just, you know—" His face twisted up in a weird scrunch of anger. "I wanted everyone to get *so* scared they were puking and pooping and when I was gone, they'd remember me and they'd feel *bad* for not liking me, and they'd always know that I got them, I *really* got them good—"

Ethan took a step back. "You did this on purpose?"

"Not the—not this part! No! I wasn't trying to get anyone hurt. I just wanted...to mess with you guys."

"You thought people didn't like you? You're, like, super popular."

"But people still hated me. Because I was rich."

"If anyone didn't like you, it's because you were a total jerk."

Kevin pouted. "No I wasn't!"

"You tried to get the whole sixth grade to fear-poop themselves as some kind of revenge! Seriously? That's a jerk move." Ethan crossed his arms. "And why would you want them to do all of that in your own basement?"

Kevin growled in frustration before blurting out, "Because we're losing this house!"

Ethan paused. "What?"

"We're not rich. Not anymore, anyway. I think we

were. But my dad lost a lot of money playing online poker. And my mom is leaving him. We're moving next week. He's going somewhere else. I dunno. They can't find out I did this...."

Kevin blinked back tears.

"Sorry," Ethan said. "That sucks."

"Super sucks."

"But, look—you can do something good before you go. We can fix this. The kids, the ones you invited here? They're still breathing. They're still *alive*. I heard their hearts beating. We just have to find the monster and—"

"No way."

"What?"

"No way. I'm not doing that. I'm not going anywhere near an actual monster."

"But—but you made this happen. You did this."

"Not on purpose." Kevin stiffened.

"Your stupid movie led to this. You need to help me fix it."

Kevin shook his head. "Nope. No chance."

"You suck."

"What?"

"You heard me. That's why people don't like you. Because you *suck*."

Kevin, lip twitching, stepped forward, and Ethan felt fear rise up in him, the fear of getting made fun of, teased, mocked, smacked, punched, kicked—

But bigger than the fear was his anger.

This rich jerk had gotten Ethan's friends hurt. And now he wouldn't even help save them! He definitely, totally sucked.

Kevin fake-lunged at him, and Ethan flinched—but he felt something roar up inside him, something that was a combination of Olivia's confidence and Harley's chaos-monkey vibe, and he fake-lunged right back at Kevin.

The other boy flinched and took a step back.

"Whatever," he mumbled.

At that, Ethan looked around the room once more, trying not to focus on all his (headless, very headless, *oh-so-headless*) classmates. There, past the air hockey table, he saw a cordless phone on the wall. He stomped over to it and picked it up but didn't hear a dial tone. All he heard was static. He tried to dial 911, but still—

Nothing.

That's probably not good.

"Cops won't believe you," Kevin said. "I mean, whaddya gonna tell them? *Excuse me, officer, a monster ate my friends' heads. Please arrest the monster immediately.*"

"Shut up," Ethan said. He stormed back over to Kevin. "The line is dead."

"Oh."

"You think people hate you now? Just wait, Kevin. People find out what happened here, you will be public enemy number one. That reputation will follow you to wherever you go with your mother, your father, whoever, whenever."

"You don't know that."

Ethan sneered. "Well, I'd bet on it. Now come *on*. We have to do something. Their heads are gone, but they're still alive, somehow. Still breathing. We can save them."

It was clear that Kevin wasn't going to help. He stood there, angry and sad and scared, staring at the basement full of headless kids—kids who were here because of him. And there came a moment when he visibly shrank in on himself, like an act of retreat.

And that was it, Ethan knew. Game over.

But then Kevin said in a small voice, "We can save them?"

"I think so." *I hope so.*

Kevin turned away from the scene of headless carnage, back toward Ethan. Something had firmed up in him. "Fine. I'll help."

They crept upstairs together. As they did, Ethan asked in a whisper: "Olivia. She was here. But she's not now—where did she go?"

Kevin mumbled an answer, sounding irritated. "How should I know? I was in the bathroom."

"Yeah. Hiding."

"Yeah. Well. I dunno where she is."

Upstairs, Ethan called out for her a few times, whisper-yelling to see if maybe she was hiding somewhere. His whisper-yells grew louder and louder until they almost became proper shouts. Kevin shushed him, told him he'd summon the monster—but Ethan shushed him back.

Didn't matter anyway. Olivia didn't answer.

She wasn't here.

They headed to the door.

On the way, Kevin said, "We're gonna lose our heads out there."

"Shut up, Kevin."

But he knew that Kevin was probably right.

The late spring night seemed to grow colder as Ethan stepped out of the house, with Kevin trailing behind.

A wind kicked up, juggling loose mulch and lawn clippings around his feet. From here, he realized, you could see the whole town and its many neighborhoods. Dark little triangles and squares. Glowing windows and flickering TV screens. Shadows and shapes of people, distant from up here, like little finger-puppets moving this way and that. He could even see the school, out past the various neighborhoods, on the far side of town. The view would've been pretty, maybe, once upon a time. Now it just felt scary and strange. (Then again, this *was* Ethan we're talking about. It probably would've felt scary and strange before, too.)

At least now he knew *why* it felt scary and strange—

Because Screenhead was out there.

Gobbling up heads.

Out there, the monster lurked. Maybe it hunted them even now, clinging to the shadows. Traveling through the power lines, or through underground cables.

A deep pit of fear threatened to swallow Ethan as easily as Screenhead had swallowed the heads of his friends. But he couldn't let it. His friends needed him. His classmates needed him. And if that meant partnering up with Kevin Rook? So be it. Whatever it took to find Olivia and save Harley.

He just had to remind himself: *They're still alive.*

And since they're still alive, that means maybe we can get their heads back.

Ethan did not understand how.

He just had to hope it was true.

Because he needed his friends more than anything. Without them, who even was he? Just some scaredy-cat weirdo with a sketchbook tucked under his arm. Would anybody else even want him as a friend? Harley and Olivia were all he had. They'd saved him that day in third grade, and he was going to save them now.

PART TWO

SURVIVE THE NIGHT, ETHAN PITOWSKI

NINETEEN
CHOOSE YOUR OWN ADVENTURE

KEVIN ROOK STOOD THERE, TRYING again and again to call his parents. But it just went to voicemail. "They must have their phones off. You got your phone?"

"My parents don't let me have a phone."

"Then how do they track you?"

Ethan blinked. "Um. They don't. They talked about tracking me with one of those AirTag things, but then they worried it would give me cancer *or* that some stranger-danger creepazoid would use it to track me, so I just make sure I go home when they want me home."

"Whatever. Gross. Mister butt kisser. Anyway, let's go."

"Where are we going?"

"To the school."

"Why would Olivia be at the school?"

"Why would I care where she is? That's where our *parents* are."

"No," Ethan said, laughing but not in a funny way. "We're going to find Olivia. That's the first task."

Kevin scoffed. "*Bzzt*, wrong. We're going to the school and getting our parents. They'll know what to do."

"You hate your parents!"

"Yeah, because they *suck*, but they're still my *parents*. And if I *don't* go to them and tell them what happened in *their* house, I'm in deep s—"

"Wait, you want to go tell your parents? You just got done being freaked out that they were going to find out—"

"Yeah, but if I get ahead of it, maybe they won't ground me until the day I graduate high school."

"Fine, whatever, but Olivia is missing." *Humongous elephant forsythia*, he thought to himself. "And I'm loyal to my friends."

"Okay, first, nobody in our class has friends. All the kids are just...just...*there*. Nobody actually likes each other. Loyalty is a joke, Pitowski. It's all a big competition. Grades, clothes, money. It's why they make us read *Lord of the Flies*. Because it's like that."

Ethan made a face. He realized: This kid is twisted. He's had his head all goofed up somehow. "*You* may not have friends. But I do. And I need to save Harley, and to save Harley, I need to find Olivia."

Obviously frustrated, Rook growled and balled up his fists. Then he took a deep breath. "Whatever. Listen. You wanna find her, I bet *she* went to the school too, because she would go and find her parents. Right?"

Ethan wanted to be suspicious. But it was solid logic. Ethan had to admit, this *was* a parent problem. They'd know what to do. That was, like, *literally the job of parents*. To know what to do.

"Y-yeah," Ethan said. "Probably."

"Right. Good. So we go to the school."

Hesitantly, he nodded. "We go to the school." He winced. "My bike is screwed up, and school is across town. Walking could take forever."

In the moonlight, he watched a big smile stretch across Kevin Rook's face. It was like watching someone unsheathe a knife.

"We don't have to walk."

"We don't?"

"I'm a rich kid. And rich kids have *toys*."

"No," Ethan said. "No no no no no, *noooooo*."

"Yes," Kevin Rook said, already mounting the dirt bike.

"Why do you have a dirt bike?!"

"Because I wanted one."

"But we're in town! You live in the direct center of town! You—you can't drive that around here!"

Kevin Rook seemed to care very little about this point, offering only a shrug as an answer. "Hop on."

"It's dangerous."

"No duh. That's why I wanted it."

"I hate you."

"I hate you, too. Get on."

Ethan tried not to scream. He had to grit his teeth and telepathically *will* his feet to move, as if he were Professor X psychically moving whole mountains with his mind. That's how hard it was. That's how much he had to work at it. But one by one, the feet moved. And when he opened his eyes, he was sitting on the back of the dirt bike. He yelped and wrapped his arms around Kevin Rook's midsection. "We have helmets, right?"

"Ha ha ha—no, helmets are for losers."

At that, he started the bike and revved the engine.

Ethan tried not to scream again, but failed.

The dirt bike leapt out of the garage like a rabbit with

a lit firecracker under its tail. *Chugchugchugvrrrrrrm!* Ethan suddenly felt the wind in his face and the bugs in his teeth and he knew that this was it, he was going to die, he was maybe even already dead, and Screenhead wasn't the one who was going to get him, nope, it was his own stupid self for hopping on the back of stupid Kevin Rook's stupid dirt bike.

Stupid, stupid, stupid.
Ahhhhhh!

TWENTY
BAD VIBES

THE DIRT BIKE GROWLED AND lurched beneath them, giving the sense that it was an ill-tamed monster bucking and kicking and snorting and hissing. The reality, Ethan realized, was far more mundane: Kevin Rook didn't really know how to drive the dang thing. He accelerated in fits and starts, he braked too late, he turned corners too fast and too tight. It was not the dirt bike that was unruly but, rather, Rook himself.

As they rode through the suburban streets—a grid of them, mostly, with the exception of those that wound around this local park or that nearby playground—Ethan tried mostly just to hold on and not die.

(This, one could argue, was his overarching view of how to exist in the world: *Just hold on and try not to die.*)

But eventually Ethan did tilt his head and lift an eyelid.

He peered out at the town around them, as if called to do so by some uncanny discomfort burying itself in his guts.

The town was quiet.

This, by itself, was not odd. Their town was not a loud town, not really. But it always had cars driving around and people walking their dogs or pushing babies in strollers, and you always heard sounds coming from inside houses, but now...

There weren't many cars driving around.

Nobody was taking their trash out.

The lights were on. But it was like nobody was home.

That's fine, he thought. *It's just a Friday night.* Friday nights weren't busy nights, he told himself sourly, knowing full well that was totally, utterly wrong.

Just get to the school.

Everything will be fine.

Said again and again like a prayer, like a poem, like a mantra.

Everything will be perfectly fine.

Once we get to the school.

Just hold on.

And try not to die.

The school, thank the gods, looked bustling. All the parking lot lights were on. The windows glowed with the burnished gold of activity. Ethan could even see people in those windows. Parents. Teachers. *Whew*.

It really was going to be fine.

Kevin Rook was right—this was the place to go. Ethan would bet that Olivia was in there already, figuring out what was going on, marshaling the parents, and putting together a plan. He pictured her for some reason with a sword in her hand and banner behind her like she was a medieval knight, some Joan of Arc figure leading the parents into battle.

Kevin killed the dirt bike's engine. He hopped off and Ethan followed, though he found his legs wobbly and weak from holding on so tight with them.

"C'mon," Rook said, waving Ethan on. He made an irritated face. "C'mon, there's a *monster* out here somewhere, remember?"

As they headed toward the school, Ethan said, reluctantly, "You were right to come here. It was a good idea."

Kevin shrugged, ever the cool kid who didn't care if people liked him. Or so Ethan had once thought. "Whatevs. Doesn't matter anyway."

"Just take the compliment."

"Sure, cool, wow." Kevin rolled his eyes. "The *Great and Popular Ethan Pitowski* said I had a good idea. I'm gone after this anyway. And nobody cares what you think."

Ethan kicked a rock across the asphalt and, under his breath, muttered, "God, you are so whiny."

At that, Kevin moved in front of him and stood still, blocking his path. He had his chest puffed out. "What'd you say, you little crapsack?"

"I said you were whiny."

Kevin stepped closer, a balloon filling with hot air. "Say that again."

It was Ethan's turn to roll his eyes. "Are we seriously doing this right now? Kevin, I said you had a good idea, and then you whined about it. We're about to go into the school and end all this—or at least, I dunno, hand the problem over to our parents. A problem that you caused by showing everyone that stupid movie! Just because you were mad nobody liked you, even though nobody liked you because you were a *jerk*. Just shut up and let it go."

Kevin blinked.

His jaw worked.

Ethan knew: *I pushed him too far.* Fear frizzled his brain cells. *Oh god, he's going to punch me.* Ethan was about to say he was sorry—

—when the angry balloon that was Kevin deflated. Mopishly he said, "Yeah, whatever. Let's go."

And at that, they headed into the school.

Geena Davis Middle School was old. It had been around since the 1940s and was built like a bunker designed to survive some endless war. It had concrete-block walls, and every open space echoed and the whole place smelled like pool chlorine.

Ethan did not like it. It had bad vibes. It felt like a literal prison.

But today? It felt like liberation. Suddenly it felt safe, impenetrable, and home to the people they needed to find.

As soon as they went in through the front, confronted by a long and seemingly infinite line of yellow lockers and blue lockers, Ethan said, "They're probably in our homeroom," and Kevin just shrugged, arms folded tight across his chest. "Upstairs, then," Ethan added, and made a sharp right into the stairwell—a place that echoed even more than the rest of the school, a place that echoed even worse than the *gymnasium*, somehow, and every step they took greeted them again in sound many times over, *CLOPclopclopclop CLOPclopclopclop*.

Second floor. *Kachunk* went the door as they opened it.

Now: a new hallway. No lockers. A homeroom quad for sixth grade.

From the closed doors, the murmur of sound. Adults talking to adults: an easy sound to identify, because it sounded a lot like someone lecturing you about something really boring, like sinks, or lawn mower maintenance, or how to get to the mall.

Their classroom was halfway down the hall.

They hurried toward it, passing closed doors with the windows that had the cross-hatching of wire in them. Through those windows they saw various homeroom teachers talking to the gathered parents. They saw Mrs. Gretsch and her wasp's nest of hair; they saw Mr. Lawry, whose head was so bald that if it caught the sun just right, it would literally blind you; there was Miss Mosco, who moved her head like a pigeon when she talked.

In each room there were interactive whiteboards—"smartboards"—on the walls or on their easel stands, showing classwork present and future.

But as they went past Miss Mosco's class, Ethan *felt* the light change. It was just a little thing, really. A flicker in the space behind him. A faint blue wash of illumination.

He skidded to a halt. Kevin nearly ran into him.

"Hey—" Kevin protested, starting to push past.

Ethan let him. He went back to the door and peered in.

The smartboard was now a blue screen.

The parents stared at it. Rapt. Their eyes shining cerulean.

No....

Miss Mosco, however, was not looking at the screen.

She was looking at the parents. Her face a mask of confusion and concern. Her head doing that little pigeon bob as she peered closer.

Miss Mosco was a good teacher. She didn't run Ethan's homeroom, but she was his biology teacher, and she had bad puns and didn't give too much homework, which basically made her amazing by any student's standards. But even if she'd been a no-good all-bad homework-spewing teacher, Ethan wouldn't have wanted her to lose her head, so he called her name, pounding on the door—

And even though he could only see the smartboard at an angle, not dead on, he could *feel* its pull. It wanted him to stare at it. It wanted his attention, forever and ever, until he had no eyes to see because the monster had taken his head. It wanted him. It wanted *all* of them to see.

Miss Mosco turned to him—

(*Little pigeon head bob*)

—and she tried to ask him what was wrong, what the problem was—

—but she must've seen his eyes flickering toward the blue-screened smartboard—

—and Ethan could see that her face was a mix of confusion and irritation and curiosity as she turned toward the screen, *no no no please no*, and when she did, her eyes met the bright-blue glow and her limbs somehow both stiffened and slackened at the same time.

Ethan threw open the door.

But it was too late.

She was locked in place.

They all were—all the parents in this room.

My parents, he thought. They weren't here. Mrs. van Eekhout's class was one door down. Ethan yelped in fear and sped out of that room and into the hallway—

—where he found Kevin Rook standing there. Staring through the glass.

At first Ethan thought, *He's been hypnotized like the others.*

But then Kevin said, "Mom? Dad?"

"Kevin—"

Kevin opened the door.

"Wait!" Ethan called out.

Just as the school's lights flickered and went out.

The only light came from the blue glow in each classroom. And in the half-darkness, a growing sound:

Vwommmmm.

TWENTY-ONE
SCHOOL'S OUT...FOREVER!

ETHAN'S BREATH CAUGHT IN HIS chest like a trapped bird struggling to get free. His lungs burned with it. He wanted to run but couldn't. He wanted to look but wasn't able to make his feet move. He wanted to be safe and free and for this all to be over with, but no amount of wishing and hoping and praying to all the gods across space and time would make that happen.

In the blue glow, he saw Kevin Rook was gone from the hallway.

I have to help him.

Ethan willed himself to creep toward the classroom.

Where the glow throbbed like the pain of a stubbed toe.

Vwommm, vwommm, vwommmmmmm.

As he moved closer and closer to the door—almost

as if he weren't walking at all, but as if it had a magnetic *pull*, drawing him deeper—he heard a voice from inside, soft and small and panicked. "Mom. Mom. *Mommy*. Please. Okay. Please."

It was Kevin's voice.

Ethan had never heard him like that—so, well...

Scared.

And—dare he say it—human.

Ethan found himself now at the door—

Inside, the parents all sat stuffed into chairs sized for sixth graders, knees tucked under desks, arms out in front of them, fingers and hands slack like washed-up squid. He saw his own parents, sitting toward the back. Their eyeballs gone, replaced by orbs of blue. Caught in the throes of the monster's hypnosis. All the parents stared at the smartboard.

The smartboard, which was already climbing off the wall.

Like a spider, Screenhead pushed its way free, long arms and legs pulling itself forward silently. The blue screen flickered—

And became an eye.

"Kevin," Ethan hissed from the door. *"Kev. In."*

But there stood Kevin, in front of his mother, shaking her. Tears in his eyes reflecting a hint of the blue from the glow in the room. He was babbling now, just a gushing rush of panic and sadness that his mother wouldn't look away, *couldn't* look away from the monster. The glow washed over him as the monster stepped close—

"Kevin!" Ethan hissed louder now.

Kevin looked toward him. Eyes wet and gleaming.

Behind him, the giant eye of the monster screen became a mouth.

With shining, glitching teeth.

Subtlety would not do, and so Ethan ditched the loud whisper-hiss and yelled, *"Kevin, it's right behind you!"*

As the creature lurched toward Kevin with alarming speed, Kevin mouthed a word to Ethan:

"Run."

Then Screenhead pounced, arms and legs perched on the desk, its black, liquid body hunched in the air—

As it took off Kevin Rook's head.

Ethan screamed.

And Screenhead swiveled its, well, *screenhead* right toward him.

TWENTY-TWO
RUN, PITOWSKI, RUN

A RECURRING MOTIF IN MANY of Ethan's nightmares was an inability to escape whatever coming danger was fast approaching. Wolves chasing, their muzzles frothing. Or a big school bus roaring toward him, its front grill a gnashing maw of rusted teeth and a pink lashing tongue. Or a masked creep with a Weedwacker revving the mosquito-whining engine as he stomped forth in garden boots.

As whatever threat closed in, Ethan would learn that his feet could not find purchase on the slick ground, or that he was sinking into the mud, or that even as he ran forward the ground was pulling back, as if he were charging on a treadmill that was far, far faster than he was. Sometimes it wasn't running, of course. Sometimes he was trying to drive away in a little car but the engine wouldn't start. Sometimes he was trying to open a door but it was locked or the knob would fall off. No matter what it was, escape was impossible. He was always stuck, too slow, with the monster faster than he was.

And that was how it felt right now.

Ethan turned to flee—

But the floor had been cleaned and waxed, and the front of his foot skidded out behind him and he almost fell forward. Somehow he managed to catch himself with his other foot and not fall.

Behind him, the blue glow throbbed brighter.

The monster has entered the hall.

Ethan tumbled clumsily forward—

Feeling like the floor was moving against him—

It's right behind me.

He could feel the glow pushing at him like a tumbling wave.

He could feel the mouth at the back of his head.

Run, run, run.

He hazarded a glance sideways, toward the other classroom doors, as he passed them—

And in the reflection of the glass in those doors, he saw that he was right.

Screenhead was right behind him. Pulling itself along

on its long limbs, not running so much as clambering through the hallway, shadow limbs making no sound as they used the doors and lockers to haul the monster forth.

Everything seemed in slow motion. Ethan watched his own hand reach out to grab the handle of the door leading back into the stairwell. He saw in that window his own reflected face, wrenched into a rictus of horror, then washed out by the glow of the yellow teeth that descended toward his head. Hurriedly he threw his body to the side and whipped the door open.

Whonnnnng!

It clipped the corner of Screenhead's monster screen-skull.

Screenhead spun and staggered back.

Ethan slid through the half-open doorway and slammed the door shut—

Just as Screenhead's horrible mouth appeared at the window.

The mouth flickered and again became an eye.

The eye stared at him. It did not try to open the door. Maybe it couldn't—Ethan didn't know. It regarded him, pinning him with its singular gaze.

Then a curious thing happened.

The eye flickered again—another glitch, like the pixels were being pulled left and right. In that burst of strange static fluttered a cascade of images Ethan did not understand:

A ratty teddy bear. A tan suburban house with an asphalt driveway. A jar of something red, like blood, pouring into a sink. A foot crunching down on black plastic. And then, *flicker-flash*, back to the giant terrible eye. Watching. Waiting.

Then, lickety-split, the beast fled back down the hall, its fleeing shadow like a black curtain dragged behind a speeding car. It whipped back into the classroom from whence it came, drawn likely by the meals it was missing rather than the little mouse—Ethan—that had escaped its grip.

There he stood, hand on the door, shaking like an autumn leaf in a storm. He knew he should go back into the hall. He should find his parents. He should save them. But could he? Or would he just lose his head? Ethan blinked back burning tears.

But he did so buoyed by one thing, one good and hopeful thing—

Though Kevin was gone and his parents were likely lost...

Olivia was not *here*.

Which meant she was still out *there*.

And he was going to find her.

TWENTY-THREE
THE NEW PLAN

ETHAN STOOD IN THE PARKING lot of the school, his heart still racing at a gallop around his chest. He was panting and sweating and wished like anything that he had Olivia and Harley here with him right now. Worse, guilt crawled over him like a nest of spiders. He'd left Kevin Rook behind. He'd left his own *parents* behind. They were up there *right now* in the school, getting...

Well, getting their heads nommed off.

He thought about crawling under one of the cars and just...going to sleep. Weariness pulled him down like quicksand.

No. You want to find Olivia, you go find Olivia. She may need your help.

Oh, sure, said an opposing voice inside his head.

You've been oh-so-helpful so far—you ended up getting Kevin Rook and your parents eaten!

Now hold on a minute, he told himself, which was maybe weird, but whatever. *That wasn't my fault. That was Kevin's fault for getting that movie from the Monarch Theater in the first place, okay?*

Fine, the opposing voice, which was still his own voice, conceded. *You didn't make this problem. But you sure didn't fix it either.*

Whatever. He had to find Olivia.

So, she wasn't at school. Where, then, would she go?

Maybe she was just hiding somewhere. Heck, she could be hiding anywhere. In any house, store, or side street.

Or maybe she's on the moon, because the moon is very far away from Earth and Screenhead is on Earth and to be safe she'd totally escape to the moon. Okay, that one didn't make any sense at all. Ethan was definitely spiraling now—you couldn't just go to the moon.

(Though, honestly, even the moon seemed to be hiding—lurking behind a band of phlegmy clouds, as if to say, *I don't want to lose my head either. Call me when it's all over.*)

Get it together, Ethan.

But he did not have it together.

He was in full-bore panic mode.

Maybe back at the house, Kevin Rook had had the right idea. Find a bathroom, hug the toilet as if it were your very best friend, and pray it would all work out. You could even talk to the toilet. Name it. *Winchester Q. Flushington. TFF. Toilet Friend Forever.*

No! No. None of that would help, he decided.

So where, then?

Would she go to her own house? Maybe. Not sure what she'd want there. Maybe she'd…gear up like they did in movies. Break a broomstick for her weapon and throw a kitchen colander on her head for a helmet.

To the police? Nah. She wouldn't go there. Olivia always said, "The cops in this town, they're not here to help us, they're here to hassle us." And so far that was true—always giving them grief just for hanging around and being kids. Still, desperate times called for desperate measures. He figured most of the police were out already trying to help people, but he could swing by there to see if anyone would help him.

But.

But.

He wanted to find Olivia. Not the police.

And she wouldn't just run and hide.

Right?

Gah! If only he could talk to Olivia.

She would know what to do.

If only I could talk to Olivia, he thought again.

Wait, that's it.

She had a phone. He didn't, but she did. She might already be trying to text him! So he had to go home, grab his iPad, and bounce her a message. She could tell him where she was, and then they'd formulate a plan. (Or better yet, she already had a plan and was going to save the day, Olivia-style. And Ethan could just cool his heels and trust that his friend had it all figured out.)

The only problem now was—

How to get home? All he had here was Kevin Rook's dirt bike, and ha ha ha yeah no he was definitely not going to try to ride *that* demon. Ethan knew he'd probably drive it at top speed into a wall. The dirt bike was a horse he would not dare to tame.

Looked like he was going to have to walk.

◆•◆

So Ethan set off from school. It'd be a good fifteen-minute walk back to his house under the ambient halos of streetlights. The town stretched out before him, quiet and eerie—it felt like a trap. Like in a video game or a horror movie, where something was going to jump out at you the moment you took a step. The moment you thought about literally anything else, then *boom*. Jump scare.

And you got got.

He tried to steady his breathing.

He kept walking.

In the distance, he heard sirens. Far enough away. He thought, *Okay that's good, right?* Someone probably hit a telephone pole. Not that hitting a telephone pole was good! He hoped everyone was okay! It's just, that meant the sirens weren't for Screenhead, right?

The sirens went on for a while as he walked, then faded again.

The eerie quiet returned.

But his ears picked up something:

A strange, off-kilter sound—like a noise underneath the quiet. Something subsonic almost, something he couldn't quite pick out. A noise that lived in the back of his ear, behind the eardrum, almost in his mind.

He walked half a block.

Then ahead, far down the road, a pulse of blue. Then dark again.

No, no, no.

It couldn't be.

The strange signal grew just a little louder.

Vwomm

Vwommmmm

The sound from Kevin's basement.

The sound from the school.

It was the sound of Screenhead. It occurred to him now that it sounded like, well, electricity. Like the buzz of some devices as they powered on. He'd heard that sound from old lamps and light fixtures too.

Another bloom of glowing blue ahead, this time in a different house.

Then again down a side street.

It's moving.

In the distance, someone screamed.

Ethan's blood went as cold as a convenience-store slushie.

Oh, heck with this, he thought, and started to run. No more walking. He had no time. And he didn't like being out here. His legs pumped as fast as they could, past house after house, and in one with a big bay window he saw a couple on the couch, sitting like they were watching a movie, some kind of snack bowl tucked between them. The lights flickered. Did they have heads? He didn't think so. All he could do was stifle a cry and keep going.

Ethan ran harder and faster.

Ahead of him, catty-corner, he saw a flash of blue

light from another house. He saw the spidery shadows of long limbs. Thought he spied the shiny yellow teeth of a glowing mouth. *It's here. It's done at the school. It's feasting on more heads.*

And just like that—

The streetlights went out. Here on this block. Then the next. Then the next after that. Darkness cascading street by street.

TWENTY-FOUR
HOME IS WHERE THE HORROR IS

ETHAN FELT LIKE HE WAS pinwheeling through the dark, just a spinning set of limbs clumsily tumbling him through the neighborhood streets. A side stitch tugged at him like a steak knife sawing through his ribs. His heart pounded; his scalp sweated itself slick. Panting, he kept on going, not stopping for one moment even as all around him he saw the glow of Screenhead appearing over there, no, now it was *there*, wait, it was ahead of him, now it was behind him. Three houses back, then two streets over, then a half-block ahead. All the while: *vwomm, vwomm, vwomm*. The glow from houses was thrown out onto the street, and in that glow the long and languid shadow of the monster feasting.

Ethan felt lost. Was he even going the right way? He was running, but to where? Home? He wasn't sure anymore.

It was, of all things, the scent of roses that saved him. His mother was an avid rose gardener, and every year she diligently fought a tide of blights and beetles to save her precious flowers. She had roses of nearly every color, even purple, and given that it was near the end of the school year, the roses were just coming into bloom, their perfumy scent filling the air more and more every day. As Ethan bolted down the street, trying desperately not to trip on the broken, uneven sidewalks of his neighborhood, the rose scent fishhooked his nose and reeled him in—

The scent carried him home.

He slumped against the front door of his house, gasping for breath.

Opening it, he stepped into the darkness of his house.

"Hello?" he called out. Maybe, by some mad miracle, his parents were home—maybe they somehow got away. He didn't *see* their heads get chomped off, after all. He called out again. "Mom? Dad?" Still nothing.

Silence was the only response.

As for Janine...maybe she'd seen he was gone and

went out looking for him? More likely, she bailed and went home. That would be the Janine thing to do.

At least he knew his house, knew how to walk through it in the dark without stubbing a toe or tripping over something. So he crept through it, his eyes adjusting. The moon lent a hand, coming out from the cloud cover and brightening the windows with its lunar glow—

And it was then he saw her in the living room: sitting there on the couch where he had left her, phone in her hand, the screen now dark. "Janine?" he whispered, then said her name louder. *"Janine."*

Her shoulders were slumped forward.

Her one leg was folded up under the other.

And her head...

Well. *What* head?

Ethan screamed.

He screamed for a good long while.

Janine was the last sort-of-almost-adult figure he'd had left to turn to. He had to assume at this point—after seeing his parents, after seeing the school and the whole *town*—that no adults were left to help him.

And that was the scariest thing of all.

Janine the babysitter had lost her head, so in a way, Ethan lost his, too.

Ethan's screaming might've been ten seconds, ten

minutes, ten hours—he wasn't really sure. All he knew was, by the end of it, his voice had gone hoarse. As the scream left him, it was replaced by a single thought: *Oh god, what if I just called the monster??* What if by screaming, he'd summoned Screenhead? What if it had realized that there was yet another head to harvest at the Pitowski house?

Ironically, that made Ethan want to scream some more, an instinct that he had to interrupt by literally clamping his hand over his mouth.

"*Mmmmmmmf,*" he screamed behind his very helpful hand.

When that was over, Ethan took a deep breath and tried very very very very hard not to think about his parents, and how right now they were very possibly still inside the school, as headless as Janine.

And he tried very very very *very* hard to remind himself that Janine was still alive and so was Harley and so was everyone who had lost their head to the head-chomping Monster Movie Come Alive.

Which was why he had to go check his iPad.

So, upstairs he went.

Thankfully, there were no new headless people at the top of the steps. He didn't know why there would be, but he had this vague fear that everywhere he turned he would again be confronted by some new headless human being.

Ethan snatched his iPad off the bed.

He tapped the screen—

It glowed.

Further, it showed that he had received *messages from Olivia*.

"Yes!" he cheered out loud, and read them—

> ethan do not come to the party something's wrong

> REPEAT DO N O T NOT NOT NOT NOT !!! COME TO KEVIN ROOK'S HOUSE

> dude r u there gonna facetime you pls answer pls pls pls

Then: three missed FaceTime calls.

After that, she'd sent him a video message.

He couldn't tell where she was; her whole face filled the screen. Her voice was a loud whisper, and though Olivia normally talked pretty fast, now her words came out at a machine-gun clip, *rat-a-tat*:

"Ethan, dude, listen to me. Some scary business went

down and the movie was some kinda trap, okay? The movie came on and, like, all the kids got hypnotized or something, and I could see in their eyes a blue screen—I couldn't wake Harley up, and—and—and—the TV started making all these sounds, this, like, *energy* sound, but then, like, also a growl? And maybe I heard someone crying and talking, too? Boy, I don't know what's going on, but there's something out here and I'm so scared—you and me need to get to the bottom of all this and I think we start at the—"

But at that point in the video, the screen went suddenly glitchy. Her face dissolved into a spray of fattening pixels and she started to say more, but the words went glitchy too, grinding into the shriek of a panicked robot thrown into a lawn mower. And then the video cut out.

He tried to send a response message to Olivia:

> Hey where are you now? I'm home.
> I saw the monster!

The iPad waited a few seconds, but then said:

> **COULD NOT BE SENT.**

Why?

Because the Wi-Fi was down. And the Wi-Fi was down because the power was out. Ethan suppressed a fresh wave of panic and tried to figure out what to do now. How could he contact her? Oh. *Oh!* Janine! She had her phone!

Downstairs he went again, two steps at a time, almost tripping—a reckless maneuver for Ethan, to be sure, but that kind of fear was trivial compared with everything he'd been through tonight. He hurried over to the couch, skidding to a halt in front of Janine's headless form.

Grimacing, Ethan plucked the phone from her grip.

(Thankfully, her fingers were fairly slack. The way she usually had that phone glued to her hand, he'd expected he was going to have to get a crowbar to loosen it.)

He pulled up her texts, ignoring the many, many messages she was sending and receiving from what looked like literally every high school student in the tri-state area, and entered in Olivia's number, *tap tap tap...*

He used the same message he'd tried to send to her on his iPad.

But again the message waited and waited—

And still didn't go through.

Janine's phone didn't have service.

No 5G, no 4G, no 3G, not a single G.

The landline!

He'd forgotten about that because, well, who used those anymore? His mother once explained to him that when *she* was a kid, she spent all her time on the phone, but she was tethered to it by the spirally cord, and he couldn't imagine what that was like, being anchored by a giant cable. It felt primitive, like riding to school on a pterodactyl, or using a fax machine.

His father had added, "You think that's something, the remote control used to be attached to the TV with a cord too." Now Ethan just thought, *Yeah, well, did the TV also used to grow legs and arms and chase people around trying to bite off their heads?*

He picked up the cordless phone from its cradle by the kitchen and—

No dial tone.

Just a repeating busy signal.

And behind it—though maybe he was imagining this—he heard another sound too.

A soft, stuttering *vwom, vwom, vwommmm*.

And then a few little clicks and clacks, ticks and tacks.

And underneath all that, a small little voice:

"I'm making a movie."

He stifled a new scream and slammed the phone back into its cradle.

Phones were out. Monsters in the phone.

Power was out. People's heads gone.

And it was then that it settled upon him, slowly, surely, like a creeping and deepening shadow: His town was just the start. This was it—this was the end of everything. Screenhead was out there taking down the electric grid, taking out cell phones and phone service, and using the cover of darkness and silence to pulse its way into the homes of all the people and—

Steal.

Their.

Heads.

And it did it fast, too. Janine's head, gone by the time he arrived. And all around him as he ran, it was popping from house to house, *vwomm vwomm vwomm*, gobbling up its favorite meal.

But why?

And how?

And how long would it be before it was done with this buffet, having sampled all the heads in their zip code? How long would it be before it reached a major city? How long before all the major cities fell? And then what?

It was the apocalypse.

No.

It was the—

The *head*pocalypse.

Ethan sat down on the couch next to Janine.

He felt paralyzed. Behind him was a crocheted afghan from his grandmother, Meemo, which was what he'd called her when he was very little, and the nickname had stuck. (His father did not like that nickname and had demanded Ethan call her "Grandmom," but Meemo had said, "Ah, blow it out your butt, Gary. I like Meemo. It sounds *fun*." Needless to say, Meemo was a lot more fun than Dad, and Ethan was not precisely sure how his father was the child of that lady. Meemo was, of all things, a watercolor painter. Landscapes, mostly, like that guy with the big hair. Sometimes Ethan wondered if the Meemo-ness of his grandmother had skipped a generation and landed on him.)

He pulled the blanket down and wrapped himself in it.

He tried not to shiver. (He failed.)

This was where he wanted to stay. Right here. Swaddled in Meemo's blanket like a human burrito. (Okay, maybe not next to Janine's nonheaded body, exactly.) It was fine. Olivia was out there. She'd fix it. She was good at stuff. She had seen what was going on in that basement and gotten the heck out of there—somehow—before Screenhead emerged. She'd get right to the bottom of it all and have it sorted out by morning.

Unless she didn't.

Unless she couldn't.

Unless she needed his help.

The crew has to hang together or it all falls apart.

That's what Olivia had said to him on their walk home that day.

That and—

Humongous

Elephant

Forsythia.

The code phrase.

Augh.

He tossed off the blanket and bounded back up to his room, whipped his backpack up onto the bed, and yanked the sketchbook from its depths. He sat, chewing his lip, thinking—before finally grabbing a pen off the desk.

Ethan began sketching, slowly at first and without much purpose beyond the comfort it brought him. He found himself drawing the monster. Multiple versions: one where it was just the TV, others where it had the glowing eye and then the glowing mouth. He wrote down next to it: *Weakness??* Because it had to have one. Didn't it? Vampires and stakes. Werewolves and silver. Zombies, go for the head.

What vulnerability did Screenhead have?

He wrote down another question: *Where do the heads go???*

Because, like, for real, where did everyone's heads go? They left behind bodies that were still alive. Still breathing *somehow*. Almost like the heads...still existed, intact, somewhere. He wrote down: *another dimension?!*

It didn't seem possible.

Then again: None of this seemed possible, so that immediately made all of this very, very possible.

He flipped the sketchbook to a new page, a blank page.

And it stayed blank.

He didn't know what to draw next. Usually his hands felt like they were on fire, like there was always more to draw, and sometimes it felt less like making something new than unearthing something out of the dirt.

But now there was nothing left to be revealed.

He was stuck.

And alone.

And entirely lost, even in his own house.

Where could Olivia be?

How could he save his parents, his classmates?

How could he help *Harley*?

At that moment he wished he could be not like

Olivia but, rather, like Harley. Just happy and goofy and unbothered by all the nightmarish reality around him. His golden-retriever self, chasing a moth or a butterfly—

Ethan froze.

Moth.

No.

Butterfly.

Yes.

Swiftly, he began to sketch. His pen *scritch-a-scratch*ing a new image onto the white void of the page: What emerged was a building, broad shouldered and theatrical, like it was beckoning you closer. Across the marquee at the top of it:

MONARCH THEATER

That's where Kevin Rook said he got the movie in the first place. From the manager there. Alongside his drawing, Ethan wrote a sentence—

I'm making a movie.

That's what the voice on the other end of the phone had said, hadn't it?

Well, if you wanted to see a movie or talk about a movie—

The Monarch Theater was where you went.

As one final flourish, Ethan drew rays of darkness

emanating from the building. You know, for dramatic effect.

He didn't know where Olivia was. But he knew where he needed to go. He needed to chase the butterfly. He needed to go to the Monarch Theater.

Ethan hopped off the bed.

He tossed his sketchbook into the backpack, shoved the pen into his pocket. He gathered up some other supplies, too: snacks, extra pens, and markers, plus one of those miniature, souvenir baseball bats you got for going to one of the local minor-league ball games. This bat had the logo of the Garyville Gumballs on it, which was to say, a baseball with a face blowing a pink gum bubble.

Ethan hurried downstairs.

On the way out, he told Janine, "I'll get your head back," even though she probably couldn't hear him because of, y'know, the *lack of ears* thing.

Then he headed out the door to find Olivia. Because the crew had to hang together.

And let's face it—she was pretty much all he had left.

TWENTY-FIVE
CHASING THE BUTTERFLY

THE MONARCH THEATER. IT WAS one of those old—what was it his father called them? *Movie palaces.* And in a way, it had the vibe of a palace, standing tall with its broad marquee, the words MONARCH THEATER ringed by Art Deco filigree framing radial lines that came from those two words like rays of sunlight from behind a single cloud. Above the sign was a king's crown, and on each side of it a pair of regal scepters. Once upon a time, these images were all dotted with brightly colored bulbs, and while many of those bulbs were now broken, just as many remained intact—and they flickered in the gloom.

Plywood covered the front windows and the ticket booth, but light bled out from the edges of the boards. The faint glow illuminated Main Street—

But it didn't travel far. It was swallowed by darkness and a creeping fog.

It was the only light around.

Which, in a town with no power, was pretty suspicious.

Ethan felt like he was all pins and needles. Getting here through the dark—and now, this fog—had freaked him out every step of the way. The theater was a fifteen-minute walk on a good day, but through the mist and the shadows it had taken him twice that, and with every step Ethan took he had feared the monster would rise up beneath him and gobble him up like a chicken finger. By the time he was at the theater, he needed a moment just to stop shaking.

"Olivia?" Ethan asked the dark. No answer. He turned toward the theater and called her name again. Still nothing.

He turned and listened, not just for any sign of her, but for any sign of the monster. But all he heard was the eerie stillness of a town suddenly abandoned.

It didn't help. It made his stomach feel sour.

Carefully, he crept to the front doors of the Monarch—they were big, broad doors, fake gold, long tarnished by the filth of time. They were glass fronted but, like the other windows, had been partially boarded up from the inside. He gently tugged on one of the handles—

It didn't budge.

Ethan walked to the other side of the ticket booth, to the second set of doors—and his shoe crunched on something.

In the half-glow from the marquee, he saw a few glittering pieces of glass—

Immediately, he freaked out. Broken glass! That was dangerous! It could embed itself in his shoe! And then in his foot! What if the *tiniest shard of glass*, like, say, an eensy glass splinter, worked its way into the sole of his foot and then got into his bloodstream and fired through his arterial network to his heart or his brain and then—well, that would be it for him, right? Lights out, kaputski.

He could practically hear Olivia's voice chastising him: *Ethan, dude, you're trying to fight a TV-headed monster. I think you can handle stepping on some broken glass in your sneakers.*

Phantom Olivia had a good point.

He stooped down a little, saw that the glass in the bottom half of the door had been broken. Beyond it waited plywood boards, but these boards didn't seem attached? Wincing, Ethan reached out and poked the plywood—and the board, held there by nothing, fell over, *kerplunk*. Light spilled out. Someone had framed out all the glass around the edge, creating a neat hole through which he could pass—and they must've propped the plywood back in place. Now the way was clear; the lobby awaited.

Could Olivia have done this?

Maybe.

Okay, he thought, *we're doing this.*

And he didn't budge.

I said we're doing this.

Still no budging.

It was as if his feet were rebelling against him. He growled and stomped his one foot down on his other foot, and that seemed to do the trick.

His body unfroze entirely and, sucking in a deep breath, Ethan chucked his bookbag through the open space—

And crawled through after it, unsure what he would find inside.

The first thing that hit him was the smell of buttered popcorn.

It was not an old smell.

It was *fresh*. And, perhaps predictably, it made his stomach growl.

Someone's been in here. The manager, he hoped.

Ahead, one long room awaited, cast in golds and reds.

A literal red carpet led to staircases on the left and on the right, each heading to one of the two theaters contained here. If you kept going straight, the lobby dead-ended at a grand snack bar. Above, light emerged from great golden disks, and along the walls were photo portraits of old movie stars interspersed with stills showing scenes from movies that Ethan had never seen, or even heard of. He stepped forward, past the black-and-white photo of a smolderingly handsome actor with an arched eyebrow and a mustache that looked carefully drawn on by a black Prismacolor marker. On the other side: a poster for a dire old French film called *La belle de la fabrique de saucisses*. The bell of the fabricated sauce? (Ethan didn't know French.)

Again the smell of buttered popcorn. It drew him deeper.

Ethan hadn't been here since...well, forever. In fact, he'd only been here once before, when his parents took him to see something his mother called "an old screwball comedy." He'd forgotten the name of it, but it was maybe three or four years ago, and it was about a dapper fella in a tuxedo and a snippy heiress who—and here Ethan's memory got a little foggy—had to hide a valuable orangutan from malicious zookeepers? And they pretended the orangutan was their adopted son? His parents thought it was the funniest thing in the world, but Ethan just thought it was kinda cringe.

Thing was, it just occurred to him: This place had been closed for over a year, but it looked brand-new. Wasn't a speck of dust on anything. No cobwebs hanging in the lights above or from any of the gilded poster frames. It didn't smell dusty or musty. It just smelled like—well, popcorn. (And maybe a little glass cleaner.)

The whole place was pristine. Someone was keeping it that way.

Ethan didn't know much about the place—why had it closed? Sometimes places closed up and shut down and it's not like they called him to explain it. And in this case he wasn't sure it really mattered.

Unless it had something to do with a monster....

"Hello?" he called out.

All that answered was the faint humming of the lights above.

"Olivia?"

Nope.

Ethan stepped forward toward the snack counter. He let his bookbag slip off his shoulder as he put his hands on the glass and stared down into its depths—

It was full of snacks.

Crunch bars and Sour Patch Kids, but also stuff he'd

never heard of: Flix Bars and Cocoa Doohickeys and something called Wallace's Licorice & Peanut Surprise. Again his stomach rumbled and he wondered: *Could I have one of these?* He knew the answer was no. These were not his snacks, and Ethan was not the kind of person to steal, both because he was a good person and because he was very much afraid of the consequences.

I don't want to go to jail over a stolen pack of Cocoa Doohickeys.

Even though he was really, *really* hungry.

Maybe just a taste—

After all, he could maybe pay the manager back later?

At that, he turned to look for the way into the snack case but couldn't even find a little door that took you behind the counter. The door that accessed that space was on the wall behind the case, which meant you had to go into some other door first. Unless, of course, he just climbed over the glass—

Which he knew he shouldn't do.

Wouldn't do.

Probably.

Right?

His tummy rumbled.

Okay, I'm going to climb over. He'd just have to be careful. The glass was probably not meant to support the weight of a human being, though Olivia always said he probably weighed about fifteen pounds soaking wet.

He reached toward the case—

And he heard the scuff of a shoe on carpet to his right.

He turned and looked—

Just in time to see someone hurtling toward him, a long weapon in hand.

TWENTY-SIX
WIELDER OF THE SACRED TUBE

"AHHHH!" ETHAN CRIED.

"Ahhhhhh!" his assailant yelled.

Ethan backpedaled, and clumsily tripped over his own bookbag, falling onto his butt—

Whud!

His attacker rose above him, weapon raised—

Then stopped.

It was just a guy. Kinda nerdy. Black-rimmed eyeglasses, mussed-up curly hair, a little beard and mustache that looked more like Oreo cookie crumbs than actual facial hair. In his hand: a long reinforced-cardboard poster tube. He lowered his nonweapon weapon, letting it hang by his side.

"Oh," the guy said, blinking. He looked at Ethan, then to the backpack, then back to Ethan. "Huh."

Ethan said nothing. He could barely catch his breath.

"Hey, little man," the guy said. He looked confused. "I know you?"

"N-no."

"Oh. Okay." It was at this point Ethan saw a small name tag pinned to the guy's white button-down shirt: ABE, MANAGER. "Um. Whaddya doing here?"

"I, uhhh." He wasn't sure how much to say, not yet. He wanted to blurt out everything—the monster, the rampant headlessness, all of it. But something made him hold his tongue. Instead he said: "Looking for someone. A—a friend."

A confused smirk from Manager Abe. "I don't think your friend is here."

"Her name is Olivia—she's my age, got braces—"

"I think I'd know if there was another kid in here." He said it kind of smug, like the way a college student taking fancy classes about dead philosophers sounds.

"Well. I thought maybe she came here."

"*Well*. She didn't."

"Who broke the glass in the front door?"

The guy shrugged. "I don't know. The alarm went off, and when I got here, it was busted out."

"Then maybe she's still in here somewhere."

Abe, the manager, frowned. He reached out a hand to help Ethan up. "Like I said, I think I'd know. It's not like this place is huge, and I checked it all out."

"It's just—"

"You should probably head home, kid. It's getting late."

"I can't go home. My babysitter—my parents—" His voice broke. He swallowed a lump of fear. "It's happening everywhere. All over town."

Abe arched an eyebrow. "Wh...what's happening everywhere?"

Oh no.

"You really don't know."

"Really don't know what?"

"About the monster."

"Monster? Monsters aren't real, little man."

Ethan hugged himself tight, the image of the dread dark thing wolfing down the heads of his friends and classmates flashing behind his eyes.

"This one is. And I think...you helped unleash it."

TWENTY-SEVEN
THE TALE OF THE TAPE

TO HIS CREDIT, ABE DIDN'T laugh or freak out or just dismiss Ethan outright. Instead, he offered Ethan some popcorn and candy, and together they went to the manager's office. The office itself wasn't much more than a glorified supply closet, replete with shelves of actual supplies: film-projector parts, boxes of chocolate bars and gummy candies, big plastic jugs of buttery goo that Ethan assumed went on the popcorn. And on the walls was more film memorabilia: posters and headshots and script pages. Not a square inch of the walls remained uncovered.

Presently, Ethan ate a Cocoa Doohickey. There were three to a pack and they looked like hockey pucks: dark chocolate on the outside, some sort of creamy milk chocolate on the inside. And something crunchy, too. It was amazing. When offered popcorn, he plunged a hand into the buttery depths and crammed some in his mouth. It mixed with the chocolate, and that became the best bite of food Ethan thought he'd ever had, and it only occurred to him after several bites that this was very, very unhygienic.

And he didn't care.

He didn't care.

His heart felt like happy birds.

But then Manager Abe said, "So what's this about a monster?"

And the happy birds all hit the windowpane of reality. *Whack.*

Ethan sighed. "You gave a videotape to a kid in my class."

"Whoa, no I didn't—"

"A horror movie."

"Oh." *Blink, blink.* Recognition dawned on Abe's face like a new day. "Yeah, right. *Demons of Death 4: Death Fingers.*"

"'The scariest movie ever made.'"

"Yeah, totally." Though Ethan wasn't sure Abe really believed that.

"Well. That movie came alive and turned into a monster."

Abe snort-laughed. But then he must have seen the dire seriousness on Ethan's face. "Wait, what? You're serious?"

"Yeah. I watched it happen."

"Monster movies don't turn into *actual monsters*, little man."

"Ethan. My name's Ethan."

Abe nodded. "Nice to meet you, Ethan." He went in for some popcorn, munched it noisily. "It's just a movie. Scary or not, movies don't come alive—"

"This one did. The TV it was on grew legs and arms and became a mouth and started eating everyone's heads, and then I think it went through the power lines from house to house, doing the same thing to everyone. Power's out everywhere. Except here, for some reason."

"That's really weird, Ethan."

"You don't believe me."

Abe leaned back, though the room was so small, the back of the chair thudded against the wall. He scowled and readjusted. "I mean, it *is* weird, don't you think? Kind of an unbelievable story from some rando middle school kid who just wandered in here, yeah?" Abe leaned forward. "Maybe *you* broke the glass in my door, hmm?"

"I didn't! I swear I didn't!"

From the manager came a scrutinizing stare. Ethan felt like he was being picked up and cut apart by a pair of tiny scissors. Finally, Abe waved it off. "Nah, you're not the type. But seriously, maybe you should go home, okay?"

"I...don't know where Olivia is. Or where to even go. Or what to do." *Wait.* "You have power here. Maybe you have a phone that works? I could call Olivia."

"Oh, yeah, no, I think the phone lines are down."

Ethan spied an old black rotary phone at the far edge of the desk. Its base was ringed in old popcorn. "Can you check?"

Waves of irritation rose from Manager Abe like heat off a hot road. "Sure, little man, sure."

He reached for the phone with his left hand.

He picked it up, put it to his ear, and then rolled his eyes.

"Sorry, no dial tone. All dead."

All dead. Ethan shuddered at the phrasing.

But that's when he noticed something.

"Uh-huh," Ethan said, almost dreamily. Because he wasn't really hearing the manager anymore. He was barely seeing what Abe was doing at all.

All he saw was the bite mark on Abe's hand.

A human-sized bite. Didn't puncture the skin but sure bruised the heck out of it. *Like a bite from someone with Invisalign braces.*

Olivia.

Ethan's pulse jackhammered every spot in his body.

Wub wub wub wub wub.

He started to sweat.

"How, uh...," he started to ask. "How is it that you have power?"

"Huh?" Abe asked.

"You have electricity when nobody else does."

"Oh. We have a generator."

Ethan shifted uncomfortably in his seat, darting glances at Abe's hand. Abe noticed and put the hand down under the desk.

"If the generator is on, then you knew the power was out everywhere else."

Abe shrugged. "Generator comes on automatically."

Ethan swallowed a dry lump of fear.

"Why are you the manager?"

"What? I'm the manager because I'm good at my job—"

Ethan gently stood up. "But there is no job. This theater has been closed for over a year. You're not the owner. You shouldn't even be here."

Now Abe's gaze turned dark as his brows knitted into

a furrowed scowl. "You're asking a lot of curious questions, little man. Crazy questions. Questions that might get you in trouble. Why don't you sit back down?"

Now it was Abe's turn to stand up. The chair groaned as he stood.

"Where's Olivia?"

"Kid. C'mon now. You're being paranoid. No need to be scared."

Scared is my superpower, Ethan thought.

Then he bolted out the door of the manager's office.

TWENTY-EIGHT
THE BONK

IT WOULD BE A SHOCK to precisely no one to learn that Ethan was not exactly an athlete. His parents had never put him on sports teams—though early on he wanted to play soccer. His parents always told him, "Well, what if you fall and break a leg?" At which point his father went into *great detail* about something called a compound fracture, which was apparently a bone break *so bad* that the bone decided it did not want to stay inside your body any longer. So Ethan had not joined the soccer team, or any other team: not track-and-field, not basketball, not baseball. The most they let him join was the chess team.

All that being said, while Ethan was not an athlete...

He sure could *run*.

Running, as it turned out, was a very good way to escape things, and Ethan was a huge fan of escaping things. Bullies? A girl you liked? Roving bees? The answer was always *Run away, Ethan Pitowski*. He had honed this crucial survival skill to a sharp edge over the years, and today was no different. He was even good with running while having a heavy bookbag on his back, which he was doing right now, breaking free of the manager's office, running around the side of the snack booth, and bolting for the front doors of the theater.

He'd formulated a plan of reaching the door, pitching his bag through the hole, and then diving after it. That, he knew, might be beyond his athletic skills, but he had to hope that this, like running, fell under the category of *escaping things*.

Posters whipped past him on the left and right.

Closer, closer.

Just twenty more steps.

He heard someone behind him. Footfalls. In a hurry.

Run run run.

Ten steps now!

Then a new sound as the footfalls ceased—

A whirling hollow *whoosh* came from behind him—

Just as—*bonk!*

Something punched him dully in the back of his

head. It hurt, and as he saw stars collide behind his eyes, his foot shifted, his ankle twisted, and the weight of his bookbag turned his body just so. And with that?

Ethan tumbled to the floor.

The poster tube rolled on the carpet next to him.

That must've been what hit him. Thrown like a boomerang or something.

Abe stepped forward and stood over him, his Oreo-crumb mustache glistening with the sweat of effort. "Sorry, little man, but I can*not* let you leave."

TWENTY-NINE
REUNION, CAPTIVITY, AND A MONOLOGUE

SURE, OKAY, HE WAS CAPTURED. Yes, he was probably in grave danger. Okay, yeah, he was being dragged into one of the empty theaters.

But—

Olivia.

Olivia!

Olivia!

She was here! In the theater!

Olivia sat tied to a chair at the very front of Theater One. Projector lights shone upon her, leaving her shadow blasted onto the big, broad screen behind her. Her mouth was sealed shut behind a bunch of old film that had been spun around her head a bunch of times.

It didn't look good.

Even still—

Ethan's heart lightened at seeing her again. Life was an ocean, and she and Harley were the driftwood he clung to so he didn't drown in the dark depths. She was order, Harley was chaos, and Ethan needed both of them to feel balanced.

"Olivia!" he yelled to her as Abe the Evil Manager pushed him forward, his hands bound behind him (tied not with film but with an aggressively knotted orange extension cord).

"Mmmph! Mmmphnn!" she yelled incomprehensibly behind her gag.

Abe pushed him down the aisle toward the front, then stopped him short at the front row. "I don't have another chair for you," he said, then used his foot to pull down one of the hinged theater seats before shoving Ethan into it.

Ethan *oof*ed and landed on his side, struggling to sit upright. His shoulders burned with his hands tied tight behind him.

"You're not going to get away with this!" Ethan said.

"Oh my *god*," Abe said, scoffing. "Really? Could you be any more of a cliché? What is this, *Scooby-Doo? Frozen? Beverly Hills Ninja? You won't get away with this, villain!* And that's my cue to say, *Oh, but I already have.*" He snorted in derision. "*Bwa-ha-ha* or whatever. Besides, do you even know what the *this* that I have already gotten away with is? Huh?"

"Well—well—" Ethan stammered, "*no*. But you gave that tape to Kevin Rook and—and—*and then* you released a monster into the world, and now it's eating people's heads and—"

Abe got right up in Ethan's face. His eyes were as big as moons. The light from the projector highlighted the sweat on his brow, his cheeks, his cookie-crumb lip. He looked almost queasy and green in this light.

At this, Ethan nearly yelped. He had to suppress his cry of fear.

"The question isn't what I did. Because, yeah, I did that. And I *knew* all that stuff would happen. The real question is, *why*."

Ethan knew what Abe wanted him to ask. But he wouldn't give this weirdo the satisfaction. Instead, Ethan shut his eyes and turned away, feeling tears burning at the edges of his lids.

"Well, I'm going to tell you why, little man. Look around you. This place? This old movie palace? It's *majestic*, kid. Opulent and design-forward! Art Deco everywhere! These are temples built to honor the old gods of cinema—" And here Abe named a bunch of people Ethan did not know. Mostly French. Jean-Luc someone.

Francois blah blah blah. Claude so-and-so. "We had French New Waves and cinematic epics and grungy little horror movies. All the posters in this place? All the memorabilia? *Hand-curated original stuff.* Each an emblem of the glory days of cinema."

He paused and made a face like he'd just licked a salamander.

The manager continued:

"But then? Those big ugly metroplexes showed up. Thirty theaters crammed into one building as the oinking masses watch the latest superhero movie while shoveling greasy ballpark nachos into their rubbery faces. Didn't stop there, though, did it?" At this, Abe spread his arms wide as if to regard the breadth and depth of his disappointment in the universe. "Now, who even needs to *go* to the theater? All the streaming services—dozens of them, where we plop into a recliner and watch whatever oozing gruel we want at any time of the day. Or worse! You open Netflix, surf the available options, put on some reality show, and then watch TikTok videos till you fall asleep on the couch. All of it disposable! How far we've fallen, little man. And that's why I did it. Because the world needs to see the power of movies again. I have shown them that power."

At that, something welled up in Ethan.

Something that wasn't fear.

Or tears.

It was—

Defiance.

He turned his head slowly and said:

"A villainous monologue? And you think *I'm* the cliché."

"You little *brat*." Abe raised his arm as if to strike Ethan with the back of his hand. Ethan nearly passed out, but he held on to consciousness with a stubbornness he generally only possessed when he was avoiding doing something really scary. Now it was the opposite: In his defiance, he kept his face raised to the manager, chin up and out, mouth in a sneer. Abe held his hand aloft, then stilled his breathing. "Nah, you're not worth it. You two sit tight. I'll be back."

And at that, Abe stormed up the aisle to the set of broad double doors at the top of the theater. He shoved the doors open and exited.

Where was he going?

And what was his plan?

Ethan stared at the door for far too long a time before letting out a great whooshing breath—one he didn't realize had been trapped deep inside him. As the breath rushed free, it became a babbling laugh because—*whoa!* Had he ever done anything like that before? Here he was, trapped by a madman movie manager who'd loosed a real monster onto the town, and instead of screaming and peeing his pants, he'd *acted like a total boss*. He was all like, *Boom, dropping a cool line*, and then like, *Yeah, go on and hit me, see if I care, Abe*, or more like, *Babe, am I right?* Wait, okay, no, that would've been a horrible thing to say, and he was suddenly very glad he hadn't said it. Still! He did it! He was not precisely fearless, but maybe that was okay? Maybe being scared and still doing the thing was the way?

This was new information.

As lost in thought as he was, it took him a bit to realize that Olivia was staring at him, eyes wide, eyebrows raised in fury, as she went "Mmmun! Mm me mppph!" again and again, rocking back and forth on her chair, looking madder and madder.

"Oh, right," he said. He looked down. His feet were free. Abe hadn't tied those up. Maybe he didn't have anything to tie them with? Or maybe he simply doubted Ethan's ability to escape with his hands tied behind him.

Which, admittedly, was probably a smart bet.

Ethan planted his feet and stood.

"Mmm!" Olivia muffledly mumbled.

"Yeah. Yes. Okay. I don't know what you're saying, so—I guess I need to get your mouth free first so we can figure out a plan?" Tentatively, he stepped forward into the garish white light from the projector. His shadow popped up on the screen, and for a moment it called to mind the dark, languid shape of Screenhead. "Gah!" He shrieked a little, then forced that image out of his mind and went to Olivia.

"Mmmm!"

"Right, so, my hands are tied, which means, uh, I'm going to have to, uhhh, get that stuff off your mouth somehow." He started to sweat again. "But the only way I have to grab something is with *my* mouth, so freeing *your* mouth means getting *my* mouth near yours, which is—" *surprisingly close to kissing and oh god.* And now his own mouth went spectacularly gooey and dry at the same time, like sandpaper run through a trench of Marshmallow Fluff. He started to hyperventilate. *I'm not ready for this. I don't even know if I like Olivia that way or if she likes me that way and if I do this our entire friendship will be ruined forever oh god oh god oh god.*

But once again, he should've been paying attention to Olivia, because her whole face was frowning now as she shook her head wildly before tilting it to the side as if to indicate—

"Oh!" he said. "*Oh.* You want me to free your hands."

Eyes wide, her head shake turned into a vigorous head *nod*.

Whew.

He hurried behind her chair, trying very hard not to fall over, because Ethan feared that if he did, he'd be like a fish flopping around on the beach. No way to get back up. Olivia's hands were bound with more film—which was not a very efficient way to tie somebody up, but Evil Manager Abe had used a *lot* of film, winding it around and around, through the gap between her wrists, and then around some more before knotting it.

"Okay, I...I am going to try to do this. With my mouth."

He cringed.

"Mmhmm," Olivia said.

You can do it, Ethan. You're basically awesome now.

Ethan bent over at the waist to start chewing at the film around her wrists like he was some kind of mad animal. It tasted super gross. Bitter, like he was licking a dental implement. *Yuck yuck yuck.*

He was at it for maybe thirty seconds before he started to get super lightheaded and he had to stand back up, gasping for air.

Suddenly he didn't feel so awesome.

"Mmmggh!" He could practically hear her telling him that Abe would be back soon.

"I know, I know!" he said. "Okay, new plan, I'm going to, um, sit down? Maybe on my knees and—and I'll work from there, otherwise I'm going to pass out, and that's not going to be good for *anybody*—"

"MMMMRRRGGG."

"Yes! Less talking," he said, once more imagining how she was likely chastising him right now. So he plonked down onto his knees (*ow*) and this time went for a different strategy—Ethan clamped his teeth down on the end of the film, where it emerged from the knot. Again and again he tugged on it, working to untie it. It didn't budge.

He growled in frustration.

Abe is going to be here soon.

And then he's going to—

Well, Ethan didn't know what.

But it wouldn't be good.

So again he got to work, pulling with his teeth on the knot—

But then he yanked his head too vigorously and immediately started to lose his balance—

Oh no no no no—

Ethan fell sideways like a toppling Jenga tower.

Whump.

But the film was still clamped in his teeth.

Which meant—

The knot was undone!

Already Olivia was working her hands free, then freeing her feet before standing up. She ripped the filmstrip gag from her mouth, flung it behind her, then strode over and knelt down by Ethan to untie his hands.

"You did good, dude," she told him.

"Thanks, Olivia."

"I mean, you could've done it a little faster."

"Olivia."

"It's cool." Once his hands were free, she stood and helped him up. "But we don't have time for a victory lap. We need a plan—and I think I got one."

THIRTY
OLIVIA HAS A PLAN

TRUTH WAS, ETHAN WANTED TO stop time and ask questions. Often enough, asking questions—and having the *time* to ask those questions—gave Ethan some comfort in uncomfortable moments. The answers were good at helping to alleviate his fears. (Of course, sometimes the answers were more like, "Well, sure, occasionally people lose arms and legs on roller coasters," which is precisely why Ethan would not once in his life be within five hundred yards of a roller coaster please and thank you.)

Presently, he wanted to snap his fingers, make the clock stop, and ask Olivia everything he could: What was this monster, how did it hypnotize people, why did she leave the party, and were they going to be okay?? Because things! Seemed! Real! *Bad!* And Ethan felt like finally,

finally there was an adult in the room and he could let go of the handlebars now, sure someone else would steer and pedal this bike. Okay, sure, Olivia was not an adult, and the actual adult nearby was a villainous movie-theater manager, but he trusted her to know what was up.

(Though here a little voice reminded him: *You did save her, remember.*)

(Which was interesting. Usually Ethan's little voice told him he was weak, the world was scary, maybe just hide your face under a pillow for a while.)

(It did not usually give him encouragement, did it?)

(Maybe the little voice deserved a cookie for saying something new.)

"Hello?" Olivia said, waving her hand in front of Ethan's face.

"Sorry," he said, lost to the contemplation of that little voice.

"Did you hear the plan?"

He bashfully admitted that he hadn't, and she rolled her eyes and told it to him again, ending her description with flair: "That's right, we're going to use the *movies* to defeat *the movie guy*." At that, she winced and added, "Okay, now that I say it a second time it doesn't sound as cool. Whatever. You ready?"

He asked her to hold on—since Manager Abe had

tossed his backpack into the seat at the top of the theater, he was able to rescue his sketchbook. He hastily drew out her plan, including a map of the theater, plus arrows and Xs to show their movement and placement.

"Dude," she said, impatient.

"I know, I know," he said, nodding. "I'm good. I'm done. I'm ready."

"Let's do this."

Ethan went and got in place.

There he stood, up in front of the movie screen, where Olivia had formerly been tied to a chair.

Olivia, on the other hand, scurried toward the top of the room, between the rows. She ducked down and, squinting against the bright light of the projector, Ethan saw her raise a thumbs-up.

Showtime.

And...he froze. He knew his job but wasn't exactly sure how to accomplish it. Was this what actors always talked about when they said they needed to figure out their quote-unquote motivation? Cringing a little at his own cringe, Ethan started saying, loud as he could, "Oh! Oh good! We are free! We should go now!"

...then, nothing happened.

Nothing except Olivia hissing from the darkness: *"Louder, dude!"*

"Olivia!" he bellowed as theatrically as he could—which was to say, very, very awkwardly. "We must run now! Qu-quickly! The manager is coming!"

Still nothing.

Maybe the manager had left the theater.

Maybe he wasn't ever coming back.

Maybe the monster had gotten him.

Were they safe? Were they more in danger than ever? Ethan had read this book one time—because learning about stuff was the only way he knew how to make it less scary—about this quantum physicist who theorized that a cat in a closed box was both dead and alive at the same time, and the only way you knew if the cat was dead or alive was by opening the box and checking. You only knew when you knew, and until then, the cat existed in both states of being, and he remembered then how much that had upset him, how everything was everything until it wasn't. And right now that feeling hit him full force like a fist to the gut: They were in the deepest danger and totally safe at the same time because Abe hadn't come back yet, and the uncertainty of it all was far worse than having an answer.

From the row, Olivia again:

"Lou! Der!"

Ugh.

Okay.

Louder.

Ethan did not know how to make his voice louder.

So he did the only thing he could:

He just yelled. Screamed. Incoherent gibberish.

"YAAAAAAAAAHHHHHHNNNHHHHAAAA-AAAAAWWWWW."

And then, moments later—

The double doors at the top of the theater were flung open, and there stood a panicked, exasperated, and *definitely angry* Abe the Evil Manager.

"You!" Abe barked.

Ethan yipped like a spooked terrier and knew again his role was singular here—remain where he was!—but doing so felt strange. Like, shouldn't he be running? He definitely *wanted* to run. But he needed Abe to...

Do exactly what Abe was doing.

Ethan froze in place as Abe bolted down the aisle toward him—

Just as a ropelike something lifted off the carpet in the aisle. The trip wire of unspooled film—the same film that had bound Olivia's hands—caught Abe's ankle. His arms pinwheeled. He fell forward, crying out.

Whud!

Abe hit the floor, and Olivia was fast to jump on top

of him. She used his back like a trampoline, bouncing the air out of his lungs as Ethan sprinted toward them. He dove on top of Abe as she wrenched the manager's arms behind his back. The man gasped for air from his pancaked lungs, and Olivia worked quickly to secure his arms even as Abe started to thrash like an angry dolphin. Ethan shut his eyes and just held on for dear life, trying to use his body as a counterweight to keep Abe still, clutching the back of the man's head like a flotation device. "Got him!" Olivia said, and for a final mic drop she wound some film around his mouth as a gag, just as had been done to her.

She helped Ethan up, triumphant. "Boom. We did it!"

"Mmph! *Mmmkkkggh!*" Abe mumbled with garbled fury.

"You know what happens now?" she asked Ethan.

"Please tell me it's time we get some answers."

A gleam of mischief caught in her eye like light off a nickel. "Oh yeah. It's time to *get some ding-dang answers, dude.*"

Ethan nearly fainted with joy.

THIRTY-ONE
A MOMENTARY RESPITE

ETHAN, EVER THE CAUTIOUS ONE, told Olivia, "I don't think we should rely on just film reels and an extension cord to keep him tied up," and she agreed. So she watched over Abe as Ethan went on the hunt for another way to secure the manager to the chair.

He spotted a roll of electrical tape on a shelf underneath the soda dispenser. (Ethan also checked to see if there was soda, because he was very, very thirsty, and also, his parents did not let him drink soda because it would, in their words, give him "superdiabetes." Which was maybe true, but right now Ethan was feeling rebellious and fearless and wanted to drink the *heck* out of some soda. And of course the soda dispenser was dry.)

Soda or no, the thick black electrical tape did the

trick: They wound it round and round Abe, ensuring there was zero chance of him escaping as they had.

As he screamed behind his gag and rocked back and forth, they went back up to the top of the theater, near the double doors, to talk.

"Okay, I gotta know," Ethan said, ready to burst, "just what is going on? You were at the party, you sent me a video and texts, then I went and you weren't there—then I got more messages from you and—"

"Settle down, dude, you gotta take a breath or you're gonna pass out. I went to Kevin Rook's house with Harley, right? We wanted to play some video games and eat fancy snacks and maybe guilt you into leaving your comfort zone a little bit to come see a scary movie. Except..."

"The scary movie was really, really scary."

"Well. Yeah."

"The monster movie was an actual monster."

"I guess that's also accurate." She sighed. "I had to go to the bathroom, and I found Kevin Rook in there acting all sus. Then I went back out when I heard that sound—you know, the one like power going in and out?"

"Almost like a heartbeat."

"Yeah. And when I went out, I saw everyone was hypnotized by the TV and I was like, something weird is going on. The VCR and TV were making these other sounds too. Popping and clicking. I thought I heard a little voice in there too, like, inside the TV? I swear I heard it say something to me about wanting to make a movie? I tried to wake up Harley, tried to get anyone to do anything. Tried to get Kevin Rook to come out of the bathroom, but he just shouted at me. I didn't know what else to do, so I got the heck out of there and rode my bike home. Nobody was there, you know, because parents were at the school, so I just chilled out and tried to call Harley and you and—" Here she paused. Fear seemed to ripple through her and she shuddered. "I looked outside and saw the flickering lights. I heard that weird electronic heartbeat sound too. So I went outside and—I saw the monster. In the house across the street. Whole family sitting in front of their television. I watched that *thing* crawl out of the TV and—and it ate their—"

"Yeah, I know."

"Then the other houses' TVs started doing it too, one by one, until it got to mine. I was sending you a message, but then the Wi-Fi went out, the power right after. But the TV came on downstairs. I saw the glow. Heard that sound. And I got the heck out of there. Just ran and ran until I figured I'd come here because I hoped you'd be here."

"Why did you think I'd be here?"

"Seemed like a smart thing to do."

He almost laughed. "I'm glad you're okay."

"Yeah. Me too." She laughed along with him. "And I'm glad you're all right, Pitowski."

Ethan cleared his throat. There was something in him then: a weird bubbly sensation, not unlike the soda he had failed to procure. It rose up from his toes, passed through his middle, and shot straight through his heart and stayed there, fizzing and frothing. It was so alien a feeling to him, he barely recognized it at all.

It was triumph.

"Okay, I don't want to do this," he said, clearing his throat of the awkwardness. "But I think I maybe can't help it? I *said* the movie was going to be scary and it was really, really scary. Like, real-deal scary. So, I know you think I'm usually *wrong* about this sort of thing, but it feels like, you know, I wasn't actually wrong this time. So it'd be really cool if..."

He let his voice trail off and gave Olivia an expectant look.

She received the frequency he was giving off and rolled her eyes.

"You want me to say it," she said.

"I do. I really do."

"I don't want to."

"I know. That's why it matters."

She sighed. "Ethan," she began, "you kinda maybe sorta had a point about the movie being scary—"

"No no no, those aren't the words."

"*Argh*. Okay. Okay! *Okay.* Ethan Pitowski—"

Here, his whole universe felt like it was zooming around him. All things into glorious focus. Was this what it was like to drink coffee? He bet it was.

"You were right."

Three words.

So simple. So clean. And yet he felt like he was flying.

This was the best worst day of his life.

He cackled like a mad scientist. The power! The glory! The utterly righteous *right-ness* of his being! Ha ha! Ha!

"You done now?" she asked him, one eyebrow arched so high, he thought it was about to levitate off her forehead.

"I guess."

She laughed a little. "Fine. You were right. But I also don't want you getting all high and mighty here, okay?" She leaned in closer. "Besides, the real win isn't that you were right to be scared. The real victory was that you sucked it up and got in the game. You pushed past the fear in here"—she tapped his temple—"and still did the thing you knew in here you needed to do." She then thumped his chest with the flat of her hand. "And because of that, I'm out of that chair and we have a shot at fixing this. Being brave isn't about being afraid. It's about being afraid and then doing what needs to be done anyway."

He nodded. "Yeah. I kind of just realized that too. Thanks, Olivia."

She slugged him in the shoulder. "You got it, Pitowski."

Ethan's brow wrinkled into furrows. "Hey. How'd we miss each other?"

"What?"

"When you left Kevin's house. I got there and didn't see you."

"I went out the back where our bikes were all parked, grabbed my bike, and hightailed it down past their gazebo, across the lawn. Faster way home. Shortcut."

"Ohhh. I called your name."

She looked thoughtful. "I moved my butt, dude. Was probably already gone by the time you were comin' up. Already on that bike, I bet—I went downhill pretty dang fast."

He paused. "I'm scared, Olivia."

"Me too, dude. That thing is taking people's..."

"Heads."

"Yeah. Heads."

"It got Harley?" she asked, hesitant.

He nodded solemnly. "Yeah. But he's still alive."

"Wait, what?"

He explained that their heads were gone—but, like, not *surgically* gone. Not actually bitten off. "They still have a heartbeat and, actually, it's like they're still breathing. Chest rising and falling and all that. Somewhere, their heads are still drawing breath."

"That's super weird."

"Yeah. But no weirder than a videotape movie monster Screenhead creeping around."

"I guess."

"Oh!" He told her then about when he found Kevin Rook and what he'd told Ethan.

She snapped her fingers and scowled. "So that little rich punk *was* pranking us. Or trying to."

"Turned out worse than a prank, I guess."

"No cap, huh." Slowly, she turned back toward the front of the old theater, where Abe the Evil Manager sat bound to his chair. "Guess we know all we know. Except *he* knows the rest."

"You think the manager will tell us anything?"

"No, but we have to try. It's on us."

"We can't hurt him."

"No. But I want to." A wicked smile crossed her face. "And we can make him *think* we're gonna hurt him."

"Wait," Ethan said, his own sinister smile taking over his mouth. "I think I have an even better idea." And at that, he once again got out his sketchbook.

THIRTY-TWO
THE MAN LOVES HIS MEMORABILIA

ETHAN STOOD IN FRONT OF Abe the Evil Manager as Olivia pulled the film gag out of his mouth. The manager snapped at her fingers with clacking teeth, but she handily dodged his effort and then flicked him hard in the ear as recompense. He yelped in pain.

"You're going to tell us everything," Olivia said, all smarty-pants.

Abe, returning the smarty-pants volley, said, "I al*ready* told you everything. Remember? Evil Villain Monologue? Hello?"

She flicked his ear again.

"Ow!"

"You unleashed Screenhead on us," Ethan said.

"Screenhead? That's what you're going with?"

Hurt, Ethan shrugged. "Well. Yeah."

"Ugh. Fine. Yes, I did. I already copped to that."

"Where'd you get the tape?"

"Offa eBay."

Olivia crossed her arms and frowned. "No you did not."

"Yeah, I really did. Seriously, just search *Cursed Items* on eBay and you will lose your mind at what you find. Haunted dolls, evil baseball cards...There was even an old toaster that supposedly told you how you were going to die when you toasted some toast."

"You don't toast toast, you toast bread," Ethan said.

"God, you kids are *insufferable*. Whatever. Point is, I found the tape on eBay and bought it."

"Did you know what it did or what it was going to do?"

"No. Not...exactly. I just knew it cursed those who watched it."

Olivia came around next to Ethan and stared at Abe with a gaze that could best be described as "lasers shooting out of her eyes."

"So how'd you figure out what it did?"

Here, Abe got a little cagey. "I watched the tape."

"And yet," she said, "I notice you still have your *head* attached."

A smile crept across his face. "I don't think I want to tell you any more."

Olivia and Ethan shared a look, and Ethan pulled something out from behind his back: a rolled-up movie poster.

Abe's eyes went wide. "Hey—"

"You said you handpicked all the memorabilia around here," Ethan said. "I bet it's valuable. To you, especially." With what he hoped was dramatic flair, Ethan gave the paper a shake and unrolled it. It was the poster for a 1970s French film: *Une cocotte pour chevaux*, directed by Henri Squelette.

"No no no no," Abe said, "don't you dare, you little—"

Ethan pinched his fingers together along the top edge of the poster. He started to move one hand one way, the other hand the opposite way—

A tiny tear appeared. *Kkkt.*

Abe made a sound Ethan didn't think humans could even make. A kind of animal shriek, like from a small animal—a startled squirrel, a shaken possum.

"I could tear more...," Ethan said.

"No, hey, *stop*. Please. I'll tell you what you want to know."

Olivia leaned forward. "We want to know how to *kill* it."

Abe frantically looked left and right, then back at the poster. He chewed the inside of his cheek. Ethan gestured with the poster, threatening to tear it all the way—and Abe gritted his teeth and let it spill.

"It's the case."

"The case?"

"Yeah, like—the case you keep the tape in."

Ethan and Olivia looked to each other, confused.

"Right, I forgot, you're basically uncultured babies. So, in the awesome era of the video store, to watch a movie you had to go to said store and pick out the movie, and when you did, the videotape came in a case. Usually hard plastic. About the size and shape of a hardback book. *Demons of Death 4: Death Fingers* has its own case, and that's where its power comes from. That's—that's why it didn't attack me. I had the case. If you destroy the case...you destroy the creature."

"Where's the case?" Olivia demanded to know.

Again Abe hesitated.

And again Ethan tore another small rip into the poster.

"*Okay okay!*" Abe barked, barely able to look at the poster being ripped. "It's in my office. All right? Locked drawer, desk, lower left."

"Keys?" Olivia asked.

He rolled his eyes. "In the *Jaws* mug on the desk."

"Let's go destroy us a monster," she told Ethan.

His heart nearly leapt in his chest.

This is almost over, he thought, quite wrongly.

THIRTY-THREE
BESPOKE CINEMATIC MONSTER ART

"THE HECK IS THIS?" OLIVIA said, holding up what was, apparently, the case to the monstrous movie.

As promised, the keys to the desk drawer were in the *Jaws* mug and the videocassette's case was in that drawer.

They'd expected something official looking. Like, a product put out by the movie company or the theatrical videotape distributor or whoever used to do that sort of thing. Something with official, if cheesy, graphic design and all that.

This was not what they thought they'd find.

It was a case with a plastic sleeve around it so you could put in your own piece of paper with a design or title or something.

The paper in there was yellowing a bit. Not new.

And it was entirely hand drawn.

Front, back, spine—all drawn, the words handwritten. (The *s* in both *Demons* and *Fingers* was that weird infinite-loop heavy-metal *s* everyone apparently drew on their notebooks decades ago. Ethan had seen his father doodle it in the margins of his desktop calendar one day while on a call, and when he asked about it, Dad seemed embarrassed and quickly scribbled it out. Mom had to explain later what it was.)

Ethan handed the case to Olivia, who read it aloud: "*Demons of Death 4: Death Fingers*. The scaaaaariest movie ever made." (*Scaaaaariest* was written exactly like that, with all those little *a*'s.) "Written, produced, and directed by Rocky Killdare, director of *Nightmare on Elm Street 13*, *Evil Dead by Dawn*, and *The Ghost-Eaters Club*."

Ethan said, "I don't think those are real movies."

"Yeah, no." She flipped the box over and read the back. "'In this explosive forbidden sequel to the fantastic Demons of Death series, the demons of the demonground have returned to Earth, hungry for human souls to consume—and human fingers!' And look—that last bit has, like, seven exclamation points."

Ethan looked. She was right. A bonafide bounty of exclamation.

Fingers!!!!!!!

"This is weird," Ethan said.

"No kidding."

"Was this even a real movie?"

"Dude, I do not know. But it kinda doesn't feel like it."

He took the case back from her. The front-cover art was a hand coming up out of a grave, and it was clearly some kind of monster hand—each of the five fingers dead-ended into a tiny demon face. Slit noses, pointy teeth, cross stares from angry eyes. What was weird was, none of this was in any way reminiscent of the monster itself: Screenhead. Ethan had expected that somehow, the monster in the movie had become the monster in real life. But this didn't look like that.

"This looks like a kid wrote it and drew it," he said. "I mean, the art's pretty good."

"*Pssh*, yours is better," Olivia said.

His heart fluttered with the compliment. "Wait, really?"

"Yeah, you're good. We don't tell you enough, but you got the skills to pay the bills. Better than whoever this kid was, anyway." She grabbed Ethan's sketchbook from his pack, flipped it to the most recent page—the drawing that showed a hastily scribbled Abe the Manager tied to a chair, cartoon tears hopping off his face as the two of them tore a poster in half before his eyes. "You drew this in, like, five seconds and it looks super cool. You can totally tell this is that evil goober dork."

His eyes shone.

"Thanks, Olivia."

"Don't get misty on me now, we got a monster to slay. How you figure we gonna destroy this?"

"Um. If it was the tape itself, we could just step on it. Or use a magnet—don't magnets erase, like, old-timey computer disks and tape and stuff? My dad's always telling me to keep magnets away from my iPad, even though I don't think it would actually do anything. But this is just the tape *case*. Hmm." He looked around the manager's office, found a pair of sharp scissors on the desk. "Maybe this?"

"Yeah." She grabbed them and the box, then mimicked the act of cutting it up with the scissors, frowning a little as she did so, like she just wasn't sure. But then her gaze drifted over and above it. "Maybe *that*."

Ethan turned to look.

There, in the far corner of the room, tucked next to a wastebasket?

A shredder.

"Jackpot bingo ta-da and voila," Olivia said, grinning like a fox.

THIRTY-FOUR
TIME TO SHRED(DER) THE BEHEADER

OLIVIA DIDN'T KNOW MUCH ABOUT shredders, but Ethan said he did: His father, the accountant, shredded documents all the time. (At one point he had asked his father, "Are you a spy? Is this secret evidence?" And his father had looked deeply appalled at the question, as if he would ever dare to be something so interesting as a spy or a destroyer of evidence. "No," his father had said, "they're financial documents over ten years in age." Boring.)

The device was essentially an angry mechanical mouth sitting at the top of its own special trash can. Whatever you put into it, it chewed up and barfed out—or, uh, pooped?—into its basket, all nice and shredded, ready to line a hamster cage.

The switch was at the top. Ethan flicked it on.

The shredder hummed gently. Like it was hungry.

For a moment, Ethan thought of Screenhead. *It* was hungry too. Somewhere out there. Shredding heads instead of paper. Or videotape cases. How far had it gone now? Was it even in town anymore? Had it gone beyond their borders to the next town over? To the city? It was like a demented math word problem: *How many heads could Screenhead eat in one hour?*

Ethan shuddered.

"Will it chew up hard plastic like this?" Olivia asked.

"Only one way to know."

Ethan popped open the case, slid the one side into the shredder—

It immediately started to chew.

NNNGGHHYAARRRRR

The case juddered and bucked in his hand.

FFFNGGGRRRRRRRRRFFFFF

But it did not get drawn in farther.

The edge got chewed up, as if by an irritated rabbit.

But that was as far as it went.

"I...don't think it's working," he said.

"Well. Dang."

"Yeah. Um. Maybe..." He took the case and slid out the paper that formed its cover, slipping it free of its plastic sleeve. And now he could really tell this was hand drawn. Not even photocopied from a drawing, but this— this was the original. He could still feel the gentle dents from the pressure of the pencil before the artist overlaid the strokes of a Sharpie marker. Could *see* the ghosts of the old pencil marks there. This was somebody's art. "We could shred this." But suddenly he felt terrible about it.

"Do it."

His hand paused.

"C'mon," Olivia urged him. "Shred that thing. Take it to Shred-Town."

"I...It's artwork."

"So?"

"Someone made this by hand. Lovingly, I think."

"And it's still part of the monster. Or spawned a monster or—well, who knows how it works. But you heard Evil Abe in there. We want to kill *that* thing, we kill *this* thing. Yeah?"

"We shred the paper and then...what about the case?"

"Uh. We stab it with scissors or we jump up and down on it. I dunno, dude, we'll figure it out."

Ethan took a deep breath.

The starving shredder mouth awaited.

His gut twisted up. His heart raced. Something about

this felt awful. Like maybe it was a bad idea. Ethan didn't know why. It was just a vibe.

Closing his eyes, he lowered the paper toward the shredder—

A teeny tiny vibration went up through his fingers, and into his wrist, then scurried all the way to his elbow—*bzzzvbbtt*. The paper was gone from his hands. The art was destroyed. It was now in the belly of the shredder beast.

He opened his eyes to look at his empty hands.

He kinda wanted to cry, and he didn't understand why.

Olivia snatched the now-blank videotape case, chucked it onto the carpet, and proceeded to stomp on it like it was a giant cockroach. Then she grabbed the scissors again, and though they still failed to cut the case, she was definitely *mauling* it pretty good. It looked all crumpled and dented and nicked. The case itself was twisted like someone with a broken back. It would no longer close easily. Panting, Olivia held it up like it was a dead frog.

"I think you killed it," Ethan said.

"I hope so. I feel pretty good about this."

"Me too," Ethan lied.

"Let's go show our conquest to Evil Abe, yeah?"

"Yeah."

They left his office and headed back to the theater, and all the while the sinking feeling inside Ethan's stomach only became larger, like a pit widening and growing deeper within him. A pit of dread, hungry and deep.

THIRTY-FIVE
WE DID IT, WE WON, EVERYTHING IS FINE NOW, SURELY

THANKFULLY, ABE THE EVIL MANAGER remained bound to his chair. Ethan wasn't sure how he could have escaped—given that they'd used essentially an *entire roll* of electrical tape on the guy—but he was a villain, and you couldn't trust villains, because of all their, well, *villainy*.

(And there the pit in Ethan's stomach grumbled, growing bigger.)

Olivia, on the other hand, seemed to have no dread to slow her down—she never did—and as such paraded their trophy in front of Evil Abe with great glee. She stuck out her tongue as she flapped the busted case with one hand and, with the other, tossed shredded paper into the air like she was trying to fling tinsel onto a distant Christmas tree.

"Ha ha!" she said, strutting now like a confident chicken. "We beat you. We beat the monster. No more heads for you!"

At that, Abe's chin dipped to his chest, as if anguish were settling over him. His shoulders shook. Ethan thought:

He's crying.

But then—

No.

Oh, no.

He's—he's laughing.

Abe's head lifted off his chest, and his eyes were shut tight as the laughter wracked him in great heaving guffaws. He did that kind of out-of-control laughing you do where you're wheezing and you make this high-pitched sound and you almost cry because it's so funny, like the joy is so large, it accidentally bumped into whatever buttons govern your internal sadness mechanics.

As his laughter washed over them like a great dark wave—they each stopped and took steps back.

Olivia shot Ethan a weird look. "Yo, why's that dude laughing?"

"I—I don't know." The deep pit had been bored all the way through him now.

"Hey," Olivia called to the manager. "*Hey*. Shut up. Stop that."

"*Stop that*," Abe said, mocking her. He gasped for air. "You—ahhh, hah, you precious little dimwits. You tiny, overly trusting knuckleheads."

"What?" Ethan asked in horror.

"I lied to you, little man. That case? It wasn't the source of the monster's power. It was the monster's *prison*. And. You. Just. Destroyed. It."

Olivia dropped the case and the shredded pages.

Abe went on:

"It was the only thing stopping that monster from coming back here to the Monarch. So where do you think it's gonna go next, hmmm?"

And almost as if his words had summoned it...the lights flickered.

Then they heard a distant sound coming closer:

Vwom

Vwommm

VWOMMMM

THIRTY-SIX
MISTAKES WERE MADE

"WE NEED A PLAN," OLIVIA said, her jaw firm, eyes wide.

"I—I don't think we have time for a plan—" Ethan stammered, juggling his sketchbook and pencil, almost dropping them both.

VWOM.

Evil Abe cackled louder.

"Dude! Plan!" Olivia said, her hand darting out, grabbing hold of Ethan's, and squeezing it so hard, the knuckles crunched like a sock full of gravel.

"Plans are *your* thing!" Ethan cried.

"Well, I got nothing, so now they're your thing!" Olivia shouted back.

"Okay, okay! I—I could redraw the cover—the cover to the movie, and—and we could put it back in a different videotape case or try to use the same one—" He flipped to a blank page and started to draw.

VWOMMMM.

The building shuddered.

Ethan dropped his pencil. It rolled under the seats. *Dang it!*

Evil Abe laughed so hard now, he almost knocked his chair backward.

Olivia turned to Ethan and hit him with a gaze that was like laser beams. "We need that pencil!"

"No, no, I have more, I have my others—" Ethan dropped to his hands and knees, scrambling to grab his bookbag, then poking around inside for his other pens and pencils. Olivia knelt with him and started to talk it through—

"So okay, on the cover, what? It was a hand, like, a monster hand? And each finger was a face—"

"Hold on, hold on," he said, finally fishing out a blue pencil and sliding his sketchbook in front of him. "It was a demon face," he answered, guessing.

"*Five* demon faces. Right. Cool cool cool. Director was Rocko Killdeer—"

"Rocky Killdare."

"Yeah yeah right, that's it—" She snapped her fingers, trying to remember more. "The back said—"

VWOMMMMMmmmmm.

It was so loud this time, it left Ethan's ears going *eeeeee* with tinnitus. Out of the corner of his eye he saw movement, and he looked behind Olivia toward the movie screen—

The beam from the projector at the top of the theater flickered and dimmed. The room strobed with light and dark. Abe raised his head, and each flash of light captured his face in a frozen rictus of terrible, twisted laughter. The screen seemed to shift and widen. Tendrils of shadow danced at its edges. *Not tendrils*, Ethan thought. *Fingers.* At that, the screen suddenly changed, and what was projected there was no longer white light but rather an image—

Bright blue.

Ethan caught sight of handwriting, the same handwriting that had been drawn on the box, written like some kind of FBI warning about not "copying this videotape" and something about how piracy was punishable by prison. But that message didn't last long as the words danced like worms and began to *change*, the letters shifting one by one—

And he could feel it inside his mind. Something reaching into his eyes, *past* them, to his brain, and seizing it—

It's hypnosis, he thought. *I'm being hypnotized.*

He cried out and looked away.

But in his peripheral vision...

He saw that Olivia had followed his stare.

She was looking over his shoulder.

No no, don't look—

But it was too late.

Her eyes were swirling now, flickering with the same effect they'd both seen on their friends and classmates. Dead penny eyes, caught in the tractor-beam trap of the screen.

Ethan grabbed her hand, squeezing just like she had squeezed his, not trying to hurt her, but trying to shake her free from the hypnosis. "Olivia, c'mon, please, please, *please*—" He grabbed her whole arm and shook it, but it wasn't working.

The blue projection on the screen shifted again—

And now, he saw, it was a singular eye.

Huge this time. Not constrained by the size of a single television set.

Long black shadows snaked out from the sides of the screen, crawling along the walls of the theater. Arms. Massive arms, bent and crooked. Fingers tickling the tops of the seats like someone playing the piano.

All the while, Evil Abe kept laughing—

Except now his laughs really were interspersed with tears. A bubbling fount of gushy sobs and hitching guffaws.

Ethan watched, frozen in horror, as the eyeball on the movie-theater screen flicked toward him.

No.

The screen pushed free of its mooring like an extruded rectangle of Play-Doh—and rose up behind Evil Abe.

Abe saw Ethan watching.

The manager gave a sad, weird little shrug.

"Sorry, little man," the manager said.

And then the screen turned into a mouth and bit his head off.

Ethan shrieked.

He scrabbled to sling his backpack over his one arm and, with his other, drag Olivia forcibly backward—but it was like trying to haul a duffel bag full of rocks and potatoes. She was thin but she was tall, and caught in the thrall of hypnosis, his friend was pure dead weight. But still, Ethan did not quit—he dug in deep, bending over and pulling her like a mule hauling a barge.

C'mon c'mon c'mon c'mon!

Inch by inch, he moved Olivia up the aisle—

A foot—

Two feet—

He hazarded a look behind him.

Vwommmm

VWOMMMM

The entire screen had now pressed forward, reaching out to that first row. It had no legs, only two massive arms hauling the eye-mouth-head forward. Screenhead's monstrous hands clawed at the back row of the theater, using it as an anchor to pull itself toward the two of them—

We can make it, we can make it—

The rest of the theater went to pitch darkness as the light of the screen above them trapped them in its glow.

We aren't going to make it.

Then he realized.

The rows of seats. They were high-backed chairs. But Screenhead's monster mouth was huge and flat.

It wouldn't be able to eat them there. It would be like a velociraptor trying to eat fish out of a too-small bucket.

Ethan dove into a row of seats, pulling Olivia with him with everything he had—

He fell sideways onto his shoulder; a starburst of pain radiated outward. Olivia's limp, hypnotized form fell on top of him, knocking the wind out of him. *Oof.* He struggled to suck air back into his lungs and make room for her—

Screenhead's massive mouth moved soundlessly to the space above them, its glowing teeth stretching wide.

The black chasm of its two-dimensional throat flickering and pixilating, somehow dark and yet somehow glowing. It descended toward them—

Ethan winced, crying out, pulling Olivia down to the floor just as the mouth flattened against the seat tops, the teeth snapping shut—

VWOM

Dammed by the seats, the monster mouth could not reach them.

There was barely enough room for the two of them down here, and he pulled her toward him—

Hoping to whisper to her to wake up, to break free from the hypnosis—

Oh no, oh no oh no nonono.

Olivia had lost her head. Literally.

The monster must have snapped it up at the last moment, seconds before he pulled her into the row, below the chairs—

No no no.

Ethan started to cry. This couldn't be. She was his rock, his life preserver, his safety and sanity in all of this. And if Olivia was gone and if this was all up to him—

Then it wouldn't get done.

He knew that now. Despair roosted upon him like a flock of crows. Picking at him. He clutched his bookbag to his chest as Screenhead continued to mash its flat mouth fruitlessly against the tops of the seats. Each time, *vwom, vwom, vwom*.

It was then he felt Olivia next to him, still breathing. Even though there was no head upon her shoulders. It was even weirder than when he'd realized Harley was breathing, feeling the rise and fall of her chest next to him like that. She was still alive. Still out there somewhere. They all were. All whose heads were taken by the monster.

Which meant that somewhere in that monster's mouth—

That's where they were.

Ethan looked up into the thing's gnashing, glitching maw. Smashing and biting and still unable to reach him.

And a stray thought struck him—

It's not a mouth.

It's a portal.

It took their heads *some*where. Okay, maybe into some kind of awful stomach realm, but...maybe not. Maybe his friends were all in there. His babysitter. His parents, for sure. Maybe he had to go in there too.

But not *just* his head.

What he was thinking—

What he was *planning*—

Ahhhhhhhh

AHHHHHHHHH

He knew what he had to do and he didn't want to do it, but—

Ethan cinched his backpack's straps tight around his shoulders. He crouched so that the mouth above him was only inches beyond the top of his head. His hair stirred every time the teeth clamped shut.

Harley. Olivia. Mom, Dad. Even Janine.

It took their heads.

But he was going to make it eat his whole body.

It was the only way. They were all gone. The town, gone. Maybe the state, the country, the whole world soon. He didn't know. And didn't want to find out.

So when the mouth next opened wide—

He put everything he had into jumping *up*.

PART THREE

INTO THE MONSTER!

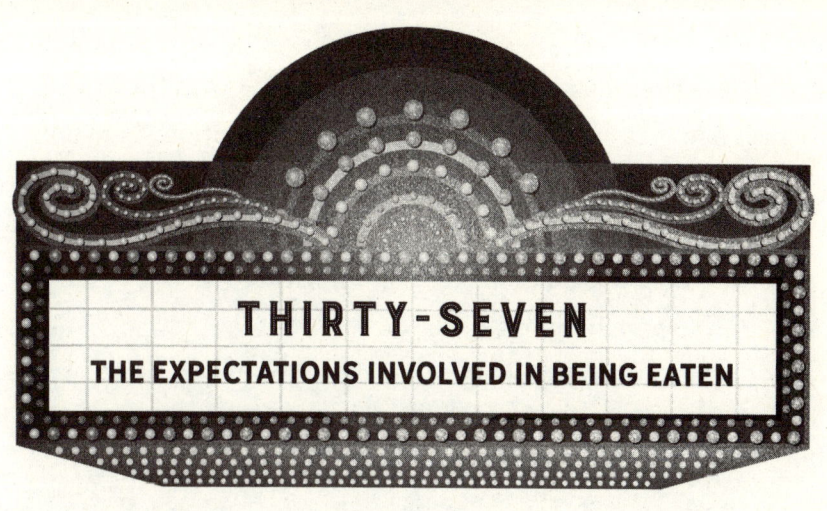

THIRTY-SEVEN
THE EXPECTATIONS INVOLVED IN BEING EATEN

BEING EATEN BY A MONSTER was quite a bit different from what Ethan had expected. Yes, there was plenty of heart racing and shrieky screaming and curling up into a hedgehog-like wad—but beyond that the experience was somehow not as bad as he thought it would be? And also much weirder?

Like, he had figured it would involve a lot of *gooey throat traversal* and maybe getting smacked in the face with some kind of giant monster uvula. Perhaps there would be a terrible smell—like old socks, rotten fruit, strange meat. If you told someone, "I got eaten by a monster," it wouldn't take long before that someone said to you, "Well, what did it *smell* like? I bet it smelled gross, like liverwurst, or foot cheese, or an unwashed mop that's been soaking in the spit of someone with the kind of bad breath that requires medical intervention." And it would be a fair guess indeed.

But there was no bad smell.

There was no esophagus damp with slime.

No punching-bag uvula.

No saliva, no phlegm, no digestive juices, none of that.

All Ethan experienced was—

Darkness.

And falling.

The fall was somehow not a straightaway plunge, either. It did not feel like a vertical drop. It felt almost like he was sliding down, as if on a hill on a sled, even though he could feel nothing underneath him at all.

Shivering, and exhausted from all the initial screaming, he tucked himself into a ball. Felt the tears burning the edges of his eyes. He clutched the straps of his backpack as if it were a life vest, but it was no such thing: He—and it—tumbled down through the darkness.

He wanted it to stop. He wished so *hard* for it to stop, making promises to the universe that were it to stop right now, he'd change—he'd be a better friend, a better son, he'd get better grades, he'd be less scared, he'd take more chances.

But he did not stop tumbling through the emptiness.

He called out, meekly: "Olivia?"

His voice did not echo. It didn't seem to go very far. Almost like he had spoken it only into his own ear.

"Harley?"

Nope.

"Anyone?"

Just talking to myself here.

Falling, falling.

Darkness, darkness.

And then—

The darkness was punctuated by a light.

Barely there, but still: a light.

A little red light. Blinking.

Way far away. Or—no. Not far. Just *small*.

And it was getting closer.

And blinking faster.

Ethan's heart raced anew. What was this? Where was he going?

A new light opened up: a circle of pale white, its edge gently spinning, the red light blinking just above it and to the right. Ethan was heading toward this new thing and he didn't want to be. Not that he wanted to remain here, forever falling through the matte-black darkness, oh no, but just the same, he didn't want to go *there*, either, thank you very much. Fear throttled him. He tried to grab something, anything, to slow his fall, but there was nothing to grab, and he plunged at an angle toward this light—which he realized now was just like the mouth. It was a portal. The mouth was the way in, and this seemed to be—

The way out.

But out to where?

THIRTY-EIGHT
DARKNESS, DEMONS, AND FABRIC SOFTENER

AND JUST LIKE THAT, ETHAN was somewhere else.

He did not land so much as simply *appear*. He did not have the feeling of falling—rather, it was like the world had rushed up to meet him where he was. *Whoosh.*

And the world was—

Well, like before, it was dark.

But *this* darkness had texture. Something in it suggested shape and dimension. All around him was a faint gradient mush of black and gray.

Further, something *else* lurked here in the darkness with him:

Scent. He could smell something—and it wasn't gross barfy smells or a foot odor or anything. It was actually kind of nice? Less *old socks* and more *new socks*. Fabric softener! Detergent and whatnot. His mother didn't use such heavily scented products, because she said they were full of "chemicals," as if the world were not literally made up of chemicals, though he supposed some of them were good and some of them were bad, like with anything. But this was a smell he smelled a lot at classmates' houses. It was a nice smell. Familiar and comforting.

It did a lot to calm him down.

He adjusted the bookbag on his back and reached out—

Instantly, he felt soft fabric. Clothes. He stood up quickly. Too quickly, as it turned out, because not only did a wave of dizziness immediately try to buckle his knees, but he *also* whacked his noggin on something. And there was a clattering rattle as some of the clothes fell around him—

The clatter was a sound he knew.

Clothes hangers.

I'm in a closet.

Okayyyy.

That, too, went against his expectations. Getting eaten by a giant monster, traveling through its void-like innards, and then getting dumped back out into a clothes-filled closet felt...

Well, it didn't feel real.

Which meant—*maybe it wasn't real.*

Or, no, maybe *this* was real, this closet. And *everything that happened before wasn't real.* No scary movie, no movie monster, no real-world nightmare. Just a regular nightmare! That was it! He must have fallen asleep somewhere—apparently in someone's closet?—and now he was waking up, shaking off the remnants of that strange and horrible dream.

(Here, though, a curious feeling struck him: a tiny little pang of disappointment. He was glad to know all that business with the monster wasn't real, of course. He wanted his friends to have their heads back. But, if all *that* wasn't real, then it meant...well, it meant his bravery in the face of such awfulness wasn't real either. He hadn't changed. He was still Ethan the scaredy-cat, the 'fraidy-boy, the cowardly kid.)

Ethan sighed. It was what it was.

He again clutched the straps of his backpack tight. *Okay, time to get out of here.*

He pawed around in the darkness, found a doorknob—

But before he turned it—

He heard something.

Footsteps.

Heavy footsteps.

Wet footsteps.

Footsteps he could only describe as *sinister footsteps*.

He froze.

Something sniffed around the edges of the door. A moist snuffling followed by a gargling hiss, like air sputtering through oatmeal. A shadow darkened the space where it was sniffling, and it was only in this moment that Ethan even realized there was a line of light ahead of him, framing the rectangle of the door.

Maybe it's just a dog.

A giant dog. A giant wheezy dog.

Like a Great Dane suffering from seasonal allergies.

Or! Or maybe it was a prank. Whoever's house he was in, they were just messing with him. Kevin Rook. It was probably just Kevin Rook.

What a jerk.

I can be brave in reality, too, Ethan decided.

He grabbed the doorknob, gave it a hard twist, and threw the door open.

"Kevin," he started, "I don't appreciate whatever it is you're—"

Doing.

The thing standing there was not Kevin Rook.

It had skin the red of spilled blood. Its arms and legs were bent at strange, impossible angles. Its head sat perched upon a long, segmented neck, and its face was a twisted amalgam of hideous features: a mouth too large for its skull, that ragged slit hosting row after row of bone-spur teeth; a pair of yellow eyes, not yellow like a cat's eyes, but the yellow of infection, of a sick liver; and a pair of rough slashes where a nose should've been were it human, which it most certainly was not.

Its mouth opened wide, wide enough to—

Bite my head off—

and a frayed, fringed tongue darted out toward him, as if to grab him. Or maybe shove itself into his mouth, or wrap around his throat.

Ethan screamed, leaning hard to the left as the fringy tongue bits seized hold of a coat hanger and drew it back toward its face with alarming speed. It was not a wise move. The coat hanger—made of thin metal—whacked it right in the eye, and it gabbled a terrible string of incomprehensible words as it staggered backward into a wall, knocking what looked to be family photos off their nails. They tumbled to the carpet as the thing swatted fruitlessly at the coat hanger.

This was Ethan's chance at escape.

He leapt free of the coat closet and saw that he had in fact stumbled into a hallway. As the demonic thing swiped at him, he darted to the right, since the monstrous hand had come from the left.

And as Ethan bolted down the hallway, he realized just what was strange about that hand. Yes, it was clad in the same blood-red skin as the rest of the demon. Yes, each finger had too many knuckles, just as the arms and the legs had too many joints. But strangest of all was that each of those fingers was topped with a little screaming demon head, each one not unlike the creature's own wretched face. Wide mouth. Teeth like fishhooks made of bone. Snapping at the air, as if trying to get a taste of his flesh.

It was the same hand that had been drawn on the videotape case.

The same hand from *Demons of Death 4: Death Fingers*.

Oh my god, Ethan realized.

I'm inside the movie.

THIRTY-NINE
DEMONS OF DEATH, IN 3D

ETHAN CRASHED DOWN THE HALLWAY, bypassing door after door, unsure where they went, but pretty sure they'd lead into dead ends like bedrooms or bathrooms. He could *feel* this new creature behind him, right on his heels, its screaming, shrieking hell fingers swiping at the back of his head.

The hallway turned a corner—he knew he'd lose momentum there, and the demon would catch him. Grunting, he let his arms and shoulders go slack so that his bookbag slid off his shoulders—

Onto the floor right in front of the demon.

It whooped a surprised hell caw as it tripped on the obstacle Ethan had dropped in its path. Ethan dared not look behind him but heard the creature sideswipe the wall, knocking down more framed photos.

Family photos that looked old.

Not, like, *old-timey* old, but retro. Ethan didn't know how to make much of an educated guess here but, what? Thirty years?

What the heck was happening?

No time to stop and think.

No time to stop and do anything.

All he could do was hard-charge forward. He rounded the corner in the hallway, nearly losing his own footing in the process—already he heard the demon behind him snarling and hissing as it clambered to its feet to continue its pursuit.

As Ethan turned the corner, he saw that the hallway ahead...

...stretched on nearly forever.

Other hallways seemed to branch off of it. There were doors. So many doors. The floor was a patchwork of carpet and hardwood. The hallway seemed to spiral, too, like it tilted to the left and kept tilting until the whole thing started to corkscrew.

It was like being in a literal nightmare. All of this was.

He couldn't stay here. Couldn't do this impossible hallway.

So he picked the first door on his left, shouldered it open, and kicked it shut behind him, clicking its flimsy lock. He fell backward, panting.

The door shuddered as the demon slammed into it.

Ethan spun his head around to look at the room he found himself in—it was like someone's old bedroom turned into storage. The walls were nearly all shelves, except for an antique sewing table across from a quilt-topped bed.

On the bed was a single old porcelain doll.

And on the shelves were...

More porcelain dolls.

Some in dirty pink dresses.

Others in gray or black dresses, as if they were in mourning.

One was definitely a clown, its bone-white face fracturing around the painted lips and starburst eyes.

The one on the bed, though...

Its dress was dark red. Hair blond, turned up in uneven, ratty tufts. Its face was bone white, and black lines like smears of coal soot had been painted around its eyes, its mouth.

Wham. The door shuddered again. The demon shrieked on the other side—

Ethan looked again to the bed. Could he grab the doll? Use it as a weapon? Maybe it was heavy enough.

Wham

Snarl, growl, froth, and hiss.

And now—

The doll on the bed—

Its head turned all on its own.

It did so with a kind of *kk-kk-kk-kkkkkk* sound. Like little bird bones flicking against other little bird bones.

Its black pinprick pupils fixed right on him.

Then the mouth wrenched open wide, and the doll screamed:

"Dead as a doll, dead as a doll!"

WHAM

The door's hinges started to come loose as the monster crashed into it once more.

"The demon is here, and soon you'll be dead like me!" the doll said, laughing as its porcelain jaw clicked closed over and over again, each click precipitating a fresh mad cackle.

At that, the door burst off its hinges—

Splinters flew.

Ethan crab-scuttled backward in a fervid panic—

The demon emerged, holding its tiny-demon-face fingers to the sky as if in a combination of both rage and triumph. Ethan knew the doll was right. He was dead. There was nowhere to go.

You gotta fight, he heard in his head. It was Olivia's voice telling him that he was brave. That he did it before and he could do it again. He told the voice okay—

And then he sprang up, arms pinwheeling frantically as he slammed himself into the demon. He reached for its face, knowing his best bet was to go for its soft parts—the eyes in particular were huge and an easy target. And if he was able to grab those and ruin the demon's sight? Then maybe he really could escape again. He cried out, grabbing the eyes even as the doll behind him laughed louder and louder, and the eyes felt like frog eggs in his grip—

Ethan dug in his fingers even as the demon grabbed him—

Then they didn't feel like frog eggs anymore.

They felt like—

Rubber.

He yanked backward, screaming as he tore off the creature's face and—

There was a human face underneath.

But not just a human face.

It was *Harley*.

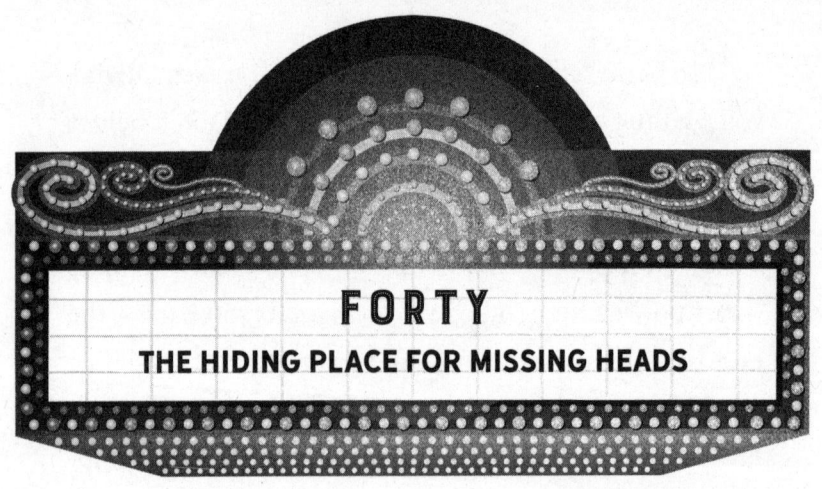

FORTY
THE HIDING PLACE FOR MISSING HEADS

"H–HARLEY?" ETHAN ASKED, FLUMMOXED.

The Harley-headed demon gave him a quizzical look like, *Who the heck are you?* Ethan was about to say something else, but then—

"Cut!"

From behind the bed, a boy emerged. Totally out of nowhere. He was roughly Ethan's age, with black hair that ran long, curling behind his ears. He had a T-shirt on from some heavy metal band called Gumdropper, and on his face a pair of big cool-guy sunglasses. In his hand: a boxy black camera. Like a film camera but also not? Like something from the olden days of the '80s or '90s—a whaddyacallit. A camcorder.

"Okay, kid," the boy said, shaking his head and popping a toothpick into his mouth. "That...that is not how this scene is supposed to go. Did you not get a script?" He looked around the room. "Did anyone give him the script?"

"I didn't give him one," said the creepy doll on the bed. A creepy doll that no longer had a dark-eyed, pale porcelain face but, rather, a very human face. A normal face. An older man, jowly. Ethan recognized him, he was sure of it.

Was that his...mailman?

Suddenly the room was awash in the babbled rush of conversation, question, and disagreement. And it came from *all* the dolls. Every one of them now wore a very real human face and was holding a porcelain mask in their tiny doll hands. "Mrs. Pepperdyne?" he asked, seeing his third-grade teacher at the end of a shelf. He hurried over. "It—it's me. Ethan Pitowski. Second row, sixth seat in? Sat next to Mary Terry, though she transferred out midyear, I think—"

Mrs. Pepperdyne had the same head of helmet hair she'd always had, like it was LEGO hair you could snap on and snap off. Not a single shellacked strand out of place. "Sorry, my friend, I don't think we know each other?"

Ahhhhhhh.

There. Four heads down. Another of his classmates! Charlie Belkin. They weren't close, and Charlie was kind of a sports kid—all the girls in class called him the "hot soccer kid" even though to Ethan's mind Charlie kind of looked like if you drew eyes and a mouth on the bucket you took to the beach to scoop sand. Which wasn't nice of him, probably. Charlie didn't bully Ethan or anything. "Charlie! It's me! Ethan! Remember? I helped you with your water-pollution project? The poster board? The cadmium?"

Charlie laughed just like Charlie laughed: a kind of *huww huww* sound, like he had last night's broccoli still stuck in his throat. "Not ringing any bells, whatever your name is."

"Ethan. I said Ethan." He spun around to Harley. "Harley! C'mon. We're, like, best friends. You, me, Olivia." He cried out his name again, emphasizing every syllable: "*Eth*-an Pi-*tow*-ski!"

Harley's eyes narrowed like he was about to remember. But then his gaze fogged over again. "Aw, man, sorry, I don't remember."

The dark-haired boy with the camera roved into view, placing himself between Ethan and Harley.

"Whoa, whoa, whoa, did you say you're Ethan Pitowski?"

"What? Yeah. Yes. What? Why?" His mind reeled. He did know who he was. But he wasn't sure how he'd gotten here. Where was he? What was this? The memory of it all was still there; he could practically feel it. In his mind, he chased it the way the demon had chased him, down a tangle of mental hallways until he caught it. And then it was there again: the giant-sized Screenhead coming off the wall in the movie theater, him deciding to jump bodily into its mouth. Then falling through darkness toward...a hallway closet.

It occurred to him: He was going to have to stand guard over his own memories, lest they be taken away. The others here clearly didn't remember him or anything else, but he remembered *them*. For now.

"Because you're here to work, my man. This is my movie."

"Your movie."

"Yeah. My movie. I wrote it. I produced it. I'm directing it."

More new information. Ethan felt his brain scrambling to decode this development. *So...I'm not in the movie.*

I'm in the making *of the movie.*

Which didn't make any more sense, exactly—but it at least meant he wasn't about to get mauled to death by Demon Fingers.

"You're Rocky Killdare." *He's just a kid, like me.*

"You've heard of me? Cool."

"I...have." Ethan wasn't sure how much to say here. Everything felt really uncertain. Like being on the thinnest of ice—one wrong step, too much pressure on your heel or toe, and *snap crackle crash*, you're down there in the deep dark cold. "I'm sorry, what movie are you making again? What's it called?"

Rocky sighed with grave impatience. "*Demons of Death* part four, *Death Fingers*. Hence the—you know." He darted out a hand, caught Harley's demon wrist, and wrenched the arm upward in order to display the fingers with little faces on them. Except now Ethan saw all those little faces...

Were human faces.

He saw that another classmate, Rachel Malinenko, was one of the fingers. The middle finger, appropriately enough. And the pinky finger was a neighbor of his, Mr. Pandher, the one who had that itty-bitty teacup poodle he took everywhere, always cradling it atop his round belly, petting it like a supervillain would.

Ethan screamed at their tiny faces.

A big smile spread across Rocky's face. "See? *Scary.* Terrifying as all get-out. You're getting what we're doing here. Scariest movie ever made! It's freaking *awesome.* Here. Come on. Walk with me. We'll talk about your job here—see if I can't wrangle up a script. You're gonna need it, after all." When he said "walk with me," Rocky didn't bother waiting for agreement. He just started moving. Ethan had to hop to a hasty jog to catch up. As they went out through the door to the hallway, he asked Rocky:

"I'm sorry, I'm gonna need the script, why? What job am I doing?"

Rocky laughed. "God, you artists really are flaky sometimes, huh? You're my storyboard guy. You're the one who's gonna draw the nightmare so I can get it out of my head—*and onto the screen!*"

FORTY-ONE
THE IMAGINARY FILM INDUSTRY, APPARENTLY

INTO THE HALLWAY THEY WENT. It was the same, but different, too. It was more garishly lit: Above them, Ethan saw strings of Christmas lights stuck to the ceiling, and in the corner when the hallway turned, he saw a flashlight mounted with a crude swaddling of duct tape. It was like everything he'd experienced running from the monster was now clearly not real.

As they walked, Rocky talked.

"We have a craft services table downstairs in the kitchen, if you can find the stairs down, am I right, ha ha," he said, as if that were a totally normal joke to make while walking down a seemingly endless hallway. "Anyway, uh, paychecks aren't going out yet, there's been a little bit of a goof-up with the bank, but hey, not to worry, we're doing this right. At least Guild minimum—" They rounded the corner and approached a lump on the floor. It was Ethan's bookbag. Rocky bent down and scooped it up. "Ooh you're gonna need this." He unzipped it, took out the sketchbook, and tossed it over his shoulder to Ethan.

Ethan barely managed to catch it, and a half-second later Rocky was pushing the rest of the backpack into his arms too.

"I don't remember, uh, applying for the job of storyboard artist. I don't even know what that is—"

"Great move, by the way—*great* move!—with the whole dropping-the-bag-in-front-of-the-demon thing. Clever. You can sub in as an actor, too, if you want. I can tell you have improv background. We need that kind of creativity, that kind of *spark*, and people who can take on multiple jobs." He lowered his voice, almost conspiratorially. The toothpick juggled between his tongue and his teeth. "Between you and me, some of the actors showing up here are not very good at this, Ethan."

"Oh?"

"Listen, I get it. This is a cherry gig. It's super rad. Anybody who is anybody will want to be a part of this. Travolta. Willis. Cruise? Probably. Streep? Most definitely. But the horror greats too. Heather Langenkamp,

Ashley Laurence, and I have it on good authority that Robert Englund has been asking his agent about us. Okay? That's how huge this is. So a lot of people want in. They want to be there on-screen when people see"—here, Rocky spread his hands out in front of him, as if imagining the movie-theater experience—"*the scariest movie ever made.*"

"*Death Fingers.*"

"Yeah, *Demons of Death 4*. You've seen the first three, right?"

"I..." *How to answer?* If his memories were already under threat of melting away, better not to confuse reality further. Besides, for Ethan, telling the truth was the most ethical thing to do, and then he didn't have to be afraid of getting caught in a lie. "I haven't."

"Oh! *Oh.* Ethan. My dawg. Those are the OGs of horror movies, okay? Like, *Evil Dead* wishes it was *Demons of Death* part one. There are demons and they're coming up out of the manholes and the toilets, and that one part with the wood chipper—and then part two with the snowplow and the primate house? Two words: demon monkeys. Am I right? But then..." His face fell. He looked almost embarrassed. "Part three. In space. Why? *Why?* So I'm fixing that crap. Make it so that people wouldn't even *remember* that there was a part three."

At this, Rocky kept walking.

Ethan trailed after, not entirely clear on what was happening.

Okay, think, Ethan. What do you know?

They were here, making a movie.

He hadn't gone back in time. Had he? Was this some kind of *Back to the Future* situation? This was clearly not reality. The hallway they were in? It was impossible, like an unending maze. Then there was the thing where, y'know, all his friends and neighbors and teachers had had their heads removed and now those heads were *here*, in this in-between place, thinking they were...actors in the movie, or props or something.

"So," Ethan said. "The other actors and crew, they just—"

Appeared, he was about to say.

But then Rocky stopped suddenly.

He held up a finger.

Ethan nearly ran into him but stopped too.

A shadow passed over them. The air grew cold.

The hairs on Ethan's neck and arms rose. Was this part of the movie? Some weird special effect Rocky had rigged up?

Rocky, too, had changed. He looked upset. Scared. Ethan knew that look. He'd seen it on his own face in the mirror nearly every morning of his life. Eyes wide. Lips tightening. That upthrust finger was now trembling.

Rocky wasn't just scared. He was *terrified*. Out of the blue, too.

"You hear that?" Rocky whispered.

"N-no," Ethan said, feeling suddenly queasy with worry.

"A door. Like a—a car door opening. It's too early. He shouldn't be home—"

"He? He who?"

Rocky's eyes glistened with fear. "The monster."

At that, the door across the hall from them popped open.

A mannequin, alive, walking, its arms and legs all janky, sprang out at them, and Ethan screamed.

It was his babysitter, Janine.

The shadows in the hallway dissipated. The lights came back up, and the tension in the air broke apart like a sandcastle hit by the sea. All of it, washed away. Rocky laughed. "Ah. Haha. *Whew*. Janine, hey, what's up."

Mannequin Janine held up a chainsaw.

"Okay, *so*," she said, her voice as disinterestedly droll as it usually was, "the SFX guys are ready for the teddy bear chainsaw scene—"

"Rad. Thanks, Janine. We'll jump to that—" Suddenly

Rocky had the camcorder in his hand again. Ethan hadn't even noticed it was gone until it reappeared out of nowhere.

"Hey," Ethan said. "Can we talk about what just happened? You said there was a monster—"

But Rocky was already going into the room, following Janine. He waved Ethan in. "Come on, man. I need you rockin' that sketchbook, yeah? I want you to sketch it out for me before we shoot—so in this scene, a teddy bear gets taken over by a demon and starts attacking everyone with a chainsaw. It's going to be *so awesome*. And we have this great new actress too—"

As they stepped into a mostly empty room—like any other room in any suburban house—another mannequin stepped into view. She wore a T-shirt, a flannel, and a pair of jeans, plus some chunky boots. When she turned around, Rocky introduced them. "This is our new actress—"

"Olivia," she said. And it was, indeed, her. Ethan's Olivia. She grinned, showing off her braces, before offering a hand. "You're the new storyboard artist, right? What's your name, dude?"

FORTY-TWO
THERE'S A TEDDY BEAR WITH A CHAINSAW

WHAT'S YOUR NAME, DUDE?

She didn't know who he was.

Harley didn't know who he was.

Ethan felt lost. Like he had gotten on a boat but forgotten to take a paddle, and now he was drifting out to sea. Land nowhere to be seen.

Rocky brought him farther into the room, had him sit behind a bed. This room looked similar in its setup to the last one: bed along the wall, shelves lining two other walls, and otherwise plain as plain yogurt. White walls, gray bedsheets, nothing that was particularly interesting or enticing about any of it. Rocky took the sketchbook out, opened it up, and paused for a moment over Ethan's art of Screenhead.

"These are cool," Rocky said with genuine awe. "*But*, save those ideas. Maybe I can use them in the next movie." At that, he hurriedly flipped to a blank page and scattered a bunch of pens and colored pencils across it. He clapped his hands. "Chop-chop, art man, let's light this candle."

All the while, the room was abuzz with movement. Rocky interfaced with Olivia and Janine and their... completely bizarre and honestly horrifying mannequin bodies. He examined the chainsaw, too, which from here Ethan could see was plastic. Just a toy for those kids who were really into, like, construction sites. It had a cord, and Rocky gave it a few test pulls—the blade's plastic teeth going *raka-raka-raka* as they spun around. Rocky then turned and handed the toy chainsaw to—

A teddy bear. Purplish, about three feet tall. Kind of ratty and beat-up looking. Had a symbol on the plain white belly: a rainbow and a sun. It had the stumpy teddy bear arms, the stumpy teddy bear legs, it had a little puffball tail, it had little half-circle ears—

But it very much had a human face.

It was Evil Abe, the Evil Manager.

Ethan stifled a panicked cry.

No no no no, not him.

Teddy Bear Abe was saying, "Thanks again for the

opportunity, Mister Killdare—I love movies so much, and I'm just so gosh darn glad to have the chance to be in a bona fide classic like this. It's a dream come true."

"Sure thing," Rocky said, giving the teddy bear some scritches behind its fuzzy stuffed animal ears. "I love movies too, kid. We all do. It's why we're here." At that sentiment, a lot of murmuring agreement went through the room. Rocky continued winding around them, holding up his fingers to make a square as if framing shots for the camera. Harley was here suddenly too—had he even come through the door? Ethan didn't remember it. Everything felt slippery and strange.

Sadness climbed through Ethan like worms through dirt. His friends didn't know him. Evil Abe was just some wide-eyed teddy bear. And all he could do was sit here and watch. Trapped.

He had to find a way out.

"All right," Rocky said, interrupting Ethan's ever-chugging train of thought. "So in this scene, our new friend Olivia is going to play Cassie, sister to Bobby—we haven't cast Bobby yet. You wanna play him?"

"What? N-no." Ethan blinked. "I have no idea what's happening."

"Okay, so, I swear the script is coming and you'll have

plenty of time to practice your lines, and truly, we have, like, *all of eternity* to get this right. Everyone in the world will wanna be a part of this movie."

All of eternity, Ethan thought. Somewhere out there, Screenhead was gobbling up the head of every last person. And those people would be coming *here*. Was Rocky the monster? Or had he created the monster and didn't yet know it?

Maybe there wasn't a meaningful difference between being the monster and creating the monster. Rocky hadn't recognized the monster, though, from the drawing....

"Rocky, hey—"

"So, you need to draw the scene—Cassie comes in, thinks everything is fine, then a demon teddy bear comes off the pile of stuffed animals on the bed and the chainsaw roars to life, *vwomm, vwommmmm*—"

The way he made those noises, they were almost like the sounds that came out of Screenhead as it appeared.

"What is this movie about?" Ethan asked.

"Demons."

"Of...death."

"Yup. Bobby and Cassie's family gets invaded by the *demons of death*, okay, and they have demon fingers and—"

Mannequin Janine called over while chewing gum: "Okay, boss, we're ready to shoot."

"C'mon, kid, draw the scene. Let's go."

Ethan hastily scribbled some of the worst art he'd ever arted. It was messy, sloppy work, the work of someone who was, well, understandably distracted by the absolute weirdness going on around him. Cassie was mostly a stick figure. The teddy bear looked a little like a melting koala. The chainsaw was more like an angry cactus than anything else. "Here."

"*Great*," Rocky said. Suddenly he had one of those clackers in his hand—the black-and-white wooden board that directors snapped together before shooting. "Action!" he barked. And just like that, the clacker board was gone—and the video camera was back in his hand. Like, *poof*. It was just there, even though it hadn't been before.

And as soon as the light started to blink on the camera—

The room transformed in a ripple of coruscating light. The walls wobbled like waves in the ocean, and Ethan rubbed his eyes as if something was wrong with them—and when he was done, the whole room had changed. No longer was it a plain nowhere nothing bedroom. It was clearly the bedroom of a teenager. Lots of black and neon colors. Posters of bands hung on the wall from groups Ethan had never heard of: Dude Crew 2000, Boy Xpress, Whoa-Town. Mounded up on the bed was a heap of stuffed animals: a pudgy horse, a poofy hedgehog, a too-long otter, and of course, in the midst of the plushy pile, a purplish teddy bear with a sun and rainbow on its belly.

Except, the teddy bear looked kinda like a koala. And it still had Evil Abe's face. He had the toy chainsaw in his hand, but sometimes the air shimmered around it—and it looked a little like he was holding a cactus.

Cassie came into the room—but it was still just Olivia's head stuck onto a mannequin's body.

"Cut!" Rocky barked, then whirled on Ethan. "Kid. *Kid*."

"What happened?"

"It's *this*," Rocky said, rapping his knuckles on the sketchbook. "You can do better. I mean"—he flipped back a few pages—"*this* is not what I'm seeing *here*." He went back to the bad koala-cactus-chainsaw art. "Let's try again. Give it a shot."

Ethan drew a breath.

Let it out slowly.

Olivia—"Cassie"—watched him. She gave Ethan a thumbs-up. Even though she didn't really remember him, she was still doing what she did best: reassuring him when he needed it. Ethan began to draw.

He went slower this time, even though it was weird having Rocky hovering over his shoulder. Taking his time helped. He laid down a light sketch framework and then began darkening it, drawing heavier lines, adding texture and shadow. The teddy bear started to almost jump from the page. The chainsaw looked like a real chainsaw—he even drew those little vibration lines around the spinning teeth of the blade to make it look like it was in motion, and for the heck of it, he licked his thumb and smudged those, too, so even the vibrations looked to be vibrating. Finally: Cassie. He drew Olivia like he knew her. Like he saw her every day. And she almost emerged from the page, fully formed.

"That's *it*," Rocky said with hissed excitement. Then he yelled: "Okay! Reset annnnnnd—*action*."

This time, *this time*—

It was different.

The door to the room opened.

Here came Olivia, dressed in loose jeans, a T-shirt, a long flannel. It was her. Not mannequin-her. But regular her, like he'd drawn her to be. She was humming a catchy pop song and then turned toward her bed.

"Wait one minute," she said, her lines practiced, and performed more than just casually spoken. "I don't remember buying you, Mister Teddy Bear."

She got closer to the bed.

Ethan wanted to warn her away—

No, run. That's Evil Abe, you're Olivia, this is all some kind of weird trap!

It was literally like being in the audience of a horror movie, wanting to yell to the main character to get away, run, don't go into that room.

It was a trap. And he'd drawn it this way.

Olivia reached for Mister Teddy Bear.

She picked him up and held him close.

"I wonder where you came from. Maybe my boyfriend Teddy bought you for me. After all, his name *is* Teddy. Or maybe my best friend Leena Patel left you here. She's always leaving something behind, that goofball. I sure know who didn't buy you: my father. He's such a jerk. Right, Mister Teddy?"

At that, Mister Teddy Bear smiled.

"Oh!" Olivia-as-Cassie-the-Sister said in practiced surprised. "You seem like a very special teddy bear."

The smile went wider.

And it had teeth.

Sharp, shining teeth.

Ethan was shocked to feel a mad thrill run through him. *I did this. I helped make this somehow. My art...* He didn't want to feel this way. It felt wrong. But he did. Like he was becoming who he was supposed to be. But also, a little—like the movie was making him into someone else. Using him like he had used it.

"What big teeth you have!" Olivia-as-Cassie said.

"All the better to eat you!" Mister Teddy said, his voice deeper and darker now—growling and glitchy.

Olivia's eyes narrowed. "You're no teddy bear."

"No!" Mister Teddy cried. "I am a *demon of death!*"

Olivia threw the bear to the bed and stepped backward—

The teddy rolled toward her, but when it stood up—

It had in its hand a running chainsaw.

A real, running chainsaw.

Yes! Just like I drew it!

The chainsaw growled as the bear revved the engine. Ethan could smell the gas fumes. This was not the same toy. Like the room, it had been *transformed*.

(*No*, he thought. *Somehow, I transformed it.*)

The teddy bear advanced on Olivia, chainsaw roaring.

But even though he'd drawn it, it was real, *too* real, all of a sudden—

Fear surged in him like it always did, with that too-much-soda feeling with the burn and the bubbles—

Ethan launched himself forward, waving his hands. "Whoa! No! Hey! Stop! *Stop.* I can't—you can't—WE CAN'T DO THIS."

FORTY-THREE
ETHAN'S INTERRUPTION IS INTERRUPTED

EVERYONE IN THE ROOM FROZE and stared at Ethan. He blinked and the weird cinema magic of the room was gone: Again it was a bland, cream-colored room. Again the teddy bear had Evil Abe's face. Again the chainsaw was a plastic toy.

Rocky stood there, jaw dropped, the toothpick dangling from his lower lip.

He eased the camera to his side.

"Kid, what the *heck*."

"I—" Ethan stammered, but he didn't know what to say. His only North Star was the truth. So that's what poured out of him. "I'm not a storyboard artist. I didn't want to be a part of this. Nobody in this movie remembers who they really are, but for some reason I know who I was before I got here." Even now Ethan could *feel* his memories trying to flee him, like cockroaches scurrying away when you flick on the lights. "I got eaten by a monster. These are people I know, and they got eaten too. And..."

They were all still staring at him.

And then they erupted into laughter.

Which was, perhaps, the most nightmarish thing of all.

Ethan felt small. And he wanted to be smaller. Had he been able to shrink himself down, down, down, until he imploded into naught but a mote of dust, he would have. But all he could do was stand there, bathed in the laughter of others. It was not the first time he'd felt this way. But given everything, it was definitely the worst of those times.

But then he noticed someone *not* laughing.

It was Rocky Killdare.

He was staring at Ethan. No, he was staring *through* him. Like there was a part of him that understood what was really going on here. Like he knew deep down maybe this movie, this place, wasn't real—or, at least, wasn't real the way he'd thought or hoped. Then: *snap*. Rocky's eyes found focus again. They pinned Ethan like an arrow to a bull's-eye, and he opened his mouth to speak—

When, somewhere in the distance, there came a noise.

A *kathunk*.

With it, the faintest vibration.

Rocky's eyes went wide. He looked at his watch, which Ethan hadn't noticed before. It was a cool calculator watch, like an artifact from the olden times, from before everyone had a supercomputer in their pocket that could also make phone calls if you really wanted to (which nobody did).

"It can't be time," Rocky said, horrified.

The rest of the room had stopped laughing.

Everyone, in fact, looked quite panicked. Their stares darting to one another, then to the door.

"What's happening?" Ethan asked.

They shushed him.

Another vibration, and another sound.

fump

fump

Fump

Fump

FUMP

FUMP

Footsteps.

Coming down the hall toward this very room.

Now Ethan felt the fear everyone else did: It was late to reach him, as first it had to run the gauntlet of his confusion. But it arrived just the same, fully formed and screaming in his ears to run, run, go, go, hide, hide. But he didn't know where to go, where to hide, or even what he was hiding *from*.

For a moment, everything was quiet.

Furtive glances passed back and forth all around the room like a silent boomerang.

Collectively, they started to relax.

But Ethan knew they shouldn't. The sound hadn't gotten quieter after it had gotten louder. No. It had stayed loud and stopped.

Right outside the door.

Ethan could see that Rocky understood that too. His guard was still up. He was shaking.

Then:

The doorknob rattled.

A shadow darkened the gap under the door.

WHUMP WHUMP WHUMP

Someone knocked on the door with a heavy fist.

Then, louder:

WHUMP! WHUMP! WHUMP!

"He's here," Rocky said, his lips quivering.

"Who?" Ethan asked him.

"The monster."

FORTY-FOUR
MONSTERS WITHIN MONSTERS

THE DOOR BURST OPEN. THE hinges clattered to the floor. Splinters sprayed as the door fell flat with a bang.

A shadowy thing stood just outside.

It eased forward with a predator's grace and stepped into the room.

Everyone screamed. Ethan included.

And the monster—

Was just a man.

He was broad shouldered and round bellied. Hair shorn to the scalp. Face speckled with beard stubble. His face strained with rage and confusion as he looked around the room, his gaze sliding over Ethan and falling on Rocky.

"This again?" the man asked, angrily.

"No, no, no, y-you don't understand—" Rocky started. "I-I-I just want to make this movie, please. It's almost done this time—just let me finish it...."

The man roared like a great beast, and his eyes turned red. Froth bubbled at his lips as he cried out, "What did I tell you? What did I tell you about all this, Robby? You know what has to be done."

"No!" Rocky cried out.

The man lifted his foot high—

And stomped it down as he stepped farther into the room.

And when he did, everything changed.

The room whirled away as if it were fabric—like it was just a set of bedsheets, or a tablecloth, whisked into the void by a yanking hand. Ethan remained where he was as the world whipped into nothing.

But it wasn't nothing. When the room was gone, something replaced it, making Ethan feel dizzy and disoriented.

Now they were in a driveway in front of a house.

The driveway was cracked asphalt, framed on one side by an unkempt hedge of boxwood. The siding of the house next to it was stained with time. The flower beds out front were weedy. But it wasn't the driveway that was interesting, or the house—it was all the pieces of stray plywood and cardboard scattered around, painted to look like monsters and popping up out of the hedge, or from behind trees or even the duck-shaped mailbox. Each monster looked familiar to Ethan, appearing to be the same demon that had chased him down the hallway—the one that was really just Harley, somehow.

Other familiar artifacts also appeared: two mannequin forms in T-shirts and shorts stood posed off to the side, one with its hands held up in front of its face (as if to say, *No, no, stay away from me, dread monster*) and another propped up against a dogwood tree in a running position. And in the middle of the driveway sat a ratty teddy bear.

It was holding a plastic chainsaw.

And then, standing in the midst of it all, Rocky Killdare.

He was there, cheeks wet with tears, cradling the camcorder to his chest like it was a lost kitten.

The man from before was here too, standing about ten feet away. He held shreds of something—long torn-up ribbons. He shook them like angry pom-poms. "I told you: No more of this junk, Robby—"

Flash.

They weren't in the driveway. They were in a child's room now. Classically messy: clothes on the floor, toys scattered across a dinged-up hand-painted dresser. One of the mannequins in the corner had a Freddy Krueger mask and glove on. The man who kept yelling at Rocky (Robby?) was ripping horror-movie posters off the wall in great swipes, the same motion you'd make if you were shaking the dust out of an old rug. Thumbtacks shot out of their corners like pebbles from the underside of a lawn mower. Ethan ducked to avoid being impaled. The man used his big, raw-knuckled hands to tear those posters into shreds.

Flash.

Back in the driveway.

"Dad...," Rocky—or was it Robby?—started to say, the rest of the sentence dying in his mouth.

"No, Robby. I told you. *I told you.* This horror stuff? It's weird. It's gross. All that mess you make—"

Flash.

The man, Robby's father, was standing over a sink, pouring out a jar of something that looked like blood—but the liquid was too bright, too red, like maybe it was fake blood, which made sense, didn't it? He emptied it into the sink while Rocky-slash-Robby stood nearby, looking both really angry and really sad.

Flash.

Back in the driveway.

(Each shift in space and time like this made Ethan's stomach do a loopty-loop like a stunt plane at an air show. He had to try hard not to yarf.)

"Dad, but I love it—"

"And it's messed up that you love it, Robby," his father said, his voice raw like grated onion. "The neighbors stare. Your teachers say you're distracted. This isn't healthy. This stuff, these awful *stories*, they're not *healthy*. Nobody wants to be scared, Robby. It's dumb. It's stupid, dumb nonsense and you know it."

"Carrie says it's good to be scared sometimes—"

Carrie. Cassie. Robby. Bobby. Was Rocky naming the characters in his movie after himself and his sister? Ethan was pretty proud of himself for making the connection.

"Your sister is leaving for college in the fall. Besides, she's a mess too. She wants to be a—a what, some charity worker? And this isn't about her, anyway! She's not your mother. Speaking of her, what do you think your mother would even say, Robby, about all this? If she were still here, she'd be heartbroken. You'd be breaking her damn heart."

Here, Robby advanced toward his father. A hopeful, almost happy look crossed his face—a ray of sun through the storm. "No, no, Mom rented me my first horror movie. She loved those movies, Dad. She got me the first *Demons of Death*—and afterward she bought me *this*."

He held the camcorder up and out. As if to say, *Don't you remember?*

The father paused. A confused look crossed his face. Shadows from clouds above drifted across them all. It was like he *was* remembering. And Ethan wanted to cheer him on: *Yes! Remember this!* He didn't know why he wanted the father to see his way to the truth, but he knew somehow it was essential.

It didn't last, this moment.

Darkness deepened the lines in the father's face and he stormed forward toward his son.

Ethan tried to cry out, tried to run in between them—

But he found his feet were stuck in the driveway. As if the asphalt had melted, turning to sticky black goo. His shoes had sunk beneath and he couldn't wrench them free, couldn't even get his feet out of his sneakers.

This really is a bad, bad dream.

All he could do was watch—

The father strode toward the boy holding out the video camera, a boy who still had hope on his face, hope that his father had remembered some core and essential truth. But then the man snatched the camera out of his hands. Robby cried out, and what came next seemed almost to happen in slow motion—the father raised the camera with one hand, like someone about to spike a football, then hurled it toward the driveway. It took forever. Plunging down, down, down, toward the hard black asphalt. The camera spiraling. Robby reaching to stop its descent. But he was too late.

The camera hit the ground—

And began to crack—still in slow motion—into pieces.

A slow, clumsy shattering. Ugly and sad.

Then, in the middle of it, everything went back to normal speed again. The camera pieces flew everywhere. Black plastic here. A bit of glass there.

The videotape—smaller than Ethan thought it would be, smaller than the one that was used to make Screenhead at Kevin Rook's house—popped out.

Perfectly safe.

Until Robby's father slammed his foot onto it.

Crunch

As soon as his foot hit the ground, a great tectonic ripple burst out. It shook the air like a sonic wave and rumpled the ground itself, a great undulation of asphalt that hit Ethan and knocked him backward. The ground cracked. The house split in two. The father bellowed in rage, his eyes turning red, his hands held aloft to the sky—each of his fingers becoming tiny versions of his own swollen, red, raw, angry face. Then all went black, and in the void a great big eye appeared above them. The eye of Screenhead.

"Stop!!" Ethan screamed, trying to wrench his feet free.

But the eye just blinked and became a mouth, then swallowed everything up.

Gulp.

FORTY-FIVE
PUTTING IT TOGETHER

FLASH.

Ethan did not expect the mouth to eat them up and then drop them here...

...in Robby's bedroom once more. Amidst the mess. Amidst the blank spaces on the wall (excepting a couple of swatches of torn horror-movie posters still stuck to the drywall with lingering thumbtacks).

Robby sat on his bed, holding the teddy bear.

He was crying softly. Just small whimpers, his shoulders shaking.

Ethan felt weird watching someone be sad. He knew he should do something, but—what? *He* was usually the one with the emotional, well, outburst. (From anxiety, usually.) It was almost never up to him to be the one to offer the hand—he was the one who took it.

So he tried to imagine what Olivia and Harley always did for him.

They always got close to him. Olivia would lean into him, and Harley usually gave him a hug if he wanted it, or made a joke. Not always intentionally, either. What else would they do for him? Well, they told him it was going to be okay, but they also never sugarcoated it. They told him the truth in a way that made it so the truth didn't hurt as much. And maybe that's all he had to do. Make the hurt...hurt less.

Ethan hopped up onto the bed, next to Robby.

He reached out a tentative hand—

This, weirdly, was scary too.

It was scary in the way that diving boards were scary, that roller coasters were scary. It had that vertigo feeling of when you're about to fall into something.

But maybe it would be okay.

He put his hand on Robby's shoulder. And the about-to-fall fear feeling went away.

"Hey," Ethan said softly.

"Hey," Robby answered.

Moments passed.

"My name's not Rocky," Robby said finally. "It's Robby Kelley. I'm not even a real director."

"Yeah, I kinda...heard that."

"You heard everything."

Ethan shrugged awkwardly. "I *saw* everything."

At that, Robby shifted on the bed, tucking into himself further. Embarrassment bloomed on his cheeks, tightening his face. "Sorry."

"It's cool." Ethan chewed on the inside of his cheek. "So, I'm guessing that was your dad, huh?"

The other boy let out a long-held breath.

"Yeah."

"What happened back there?"

"I have to start the movie over again. This..." Now embarrassment turned to a thunder rumble of anger. "This *keeps happening*. I keep starting the movie. It keeps going great. *Demons of Death* part four, *Death Fingers*, really gets cooking, it's just, awesome super-gnarly stuff, really cool, really scary. More and more actors come in. We get better effects. And just as I'm feeling happy with it, and just as we get close to the end—" He makes two fists and crushes them together. "Wham. Here *he* comes to mess it all up. Stomping into my scene. Grabbing my camera. He breaks it into pieces and"—Robby's chest hitched, like he was trying to hold back a sob—"then it's gone. My horror movie is dead in the water like Bruce the Shark from *Jaws*."

He must've felt Ethan's quizzical glance, so Robby explained: "The shark in *Jaws* was a mechanical shark and it didn't really work well, which is why Spielberg pulled back on using the shark special effect so much—which means most of the movie is shot *not* seeing the shark, which ended up actually making it way, way scarier."

"Oh."

Robby hopped off the bed. On his dresser, among the mess of knickknacks and Nintendo controllers and posed toys—

A video camera appeared.

The same one.

Robby reached for it, then mashed the rewind button, and the camera started to make a sound not entirely unlike *vwom vwom vwommm*.

"Time to start over," Robby said, and went to press another button.

"Wait," Ethan blurted out.

"What?" the other boy asked.

"I just—that doesn't feel right."

"But that's how it is. I make the movie. I get close to the end. Then *he* comes and messes it all up. I don't know why he does. Maybe he's mad about my mom. Or sad about her. Or...maybe he just hates movies." Robby suddenly had a toothpick in his mouth, which bobbled around as his tongue fidgeted with it. "But I'll finish this flick one of these days. One of these days he won't catch me. And then I'll have made"—he paused for dramatic effect—"*the scariest movie ever made.*"

That was it.

That was it.

Ethan didn't know...exactly what was going on here. How real was any of this? Was this Robby's mind? Was this some kind of weird endless videotape fake-film-set purgatory? Was this all in *Ethan's* mind? Was Robby alive or dead, or was he ever real? Ethan didn't have answers to any of that.

But he had one answer, for absolute sure.

"You already made the scariest movie ever made."

"Huh?"

"You did it. This? All of this? It...started something. Something bad, like, *really really bad*, but your movie has become this living legend. Actually, *literally* living. Like, everyone talks about your movie on the internet."

"The innerwhat?"

"The inter—oh." Right. Robby was born before the internet, and they were stuck in—what decade was this? The 1990s? Was this time travel? Ethan's head spun at the thought of that. "It's like an urban legend except real. Your videotape, your movie? People whisper about it. They tell stories about how scary it is. And it is really, really scary. Because when you put its tape into a tape player, the whole thing comes alive. It turns into this...monster. I call it Screenhead—"

"I can't tell if that's the best or worst name ever for a horror movie monster."

Ethan shrugged. "It's literally what it is, though. This TV with an eyeball, sometimes a mouth. It hypnotizes people and then...bites their heads off."

"That's the thing you drew in your sketchbook."

"Right. But here's the thing, Robby. The people whose heads it took? They're still alive. They're *here*. Olivia? Harley? The guy playing the teddy bear? They're all people whose heads were bitten off. They came through the monster to this place. Which means either the monster is a conduit, or we're in the stomach, or—"

"Or I'm the monster."

Ethan winced. "Maybe."

Robby seemed to think on this. It upset him, clearly, but not in a way where he was crushed by it. His brow knitted like he was thinking hard. The toothpick waggled frustratedly back and forth.

"Show me," Robby said, suddenly.

"Show you what?"

Robby walked around behind Ethan and unzipped the bookbag still on his shoulders. He thrust out the sketchbook. Ethan wasn't even sure how it had gotten back in his bag—just the way this dreamlike place seemed to work. "I want you to show me...y'know. Everything. The monster. How you got here."

"Huh? Why?"

The other boy shrugged. "You're my storyboard artist. Just feels right. I did the art for the tape case, but it wasn't anything like your work. When you got here, something felt different, like you were here to...help me finish the movie the right way." A sigh. "Maybe I'm a little too controlling? I want everything my way. My dad's like that too and I hate it and...I should be better, I guess. Thing is, whatever the other reason is, the bigger reason, I think let's see what that is, you know?"

Ethan didn't know if this would help anything.

But in his gut, he had a feeling it was the right thing to do. His fingers tingled with the urge to draw. Like they were coursing with gentle electricity.

Robby held out the sketchbook again. Gave it a little waggle.

Ethan took it.

"You're still gonna help me?" Robby asked.

"Yeah. But I'm going to need my pens, too."

The other boy winked and gave the toothpick a flip in his mouth. "On it, my intrepid Art Man." And at that, he rooted around in the bookbag until he found the pens. He handed them to Ethan. They, too, seemed to crackle with power. Not just electricity but something else. Something bigger.

Power. No. *Potential*.

And then, Ethan knew, it was time to draw.

FORTY-SIX
OOPS, I ARTED

ETHAN TOOK HIS PEN AND felt the power in it—not a supernatural power, not really, just the weird magical power of making something out of nothing. And so that is what he did. He sat on Robby's bed and felt his arm begin to move. His wrist pivoted. He used his one hand to turn the sketchbook this way and that, like he'd seen many of his favorite comic book artists do on YouTube. And what came out of him first was the image of the old box TV growing arms and legs, one eye scanning a room full of hypnotized sixth graders (all with their heads intact at that point). He shaded in the margins of the room and drew sharp-angled light coming from the monster's screen-face.

"Whoa," Robby said. "That's really freaky."

"Yeah," Ethan said, except a strange thing happened. It wasn't as freaky to him. Maybe not even freaky at all. It was like drawing it on paper robbed it of some of its power. It stole the fear from the moment and turned it into art.

More furiously now, Ethan drew:

The first time it gobbled up a kid's head. *Chomp.*

The time he saw it in a house as he passed, a great looming thin-bodied shadow-monster, advancing on a family sitting on their couch.

The time he found his babysitter headless, her phone still in hand.

And then he drew everything that had happened at the theater: Evil Abe tying them up, them tying *him* up, then the monster coming alive as the whole movie screen itself, a giant flat-headed hungry mouth ready to chomp, chomp, chomp.

Robby rubbed his hands over his arms. "I got goose pimples, kid."

"It was pretty nuts."

The last thing Ethan drew was—

Himself.

Jumping up into the mouth.

"That's when I came here," Ethan said, his voice soft.

"Kid, you got some juicy guts. That's rad. Totally fearless! Hero move."

"I—I'm not a hero. I just wanted to save my friends. I was really scared."

Robby clapped him on the back. "It's cool to be scared. It's why I like watching scary movies. Makes me scared in the moment but then, y'know, *less* scared later."

"That's neat." Ethan hemmed and hawed a bit before confessing: "I've never seen a scary movie before."

Robby laughed. "Well, kid, you *lived* one."

"I think I'm *still* living one."

Robby seemed suddenly worried. "So, what is this place? Is it real? Am I real?" His cheeks went white. "Am I alive?"

"I don't know. But I think so."

"I think so too." Robby checked his own pulse. "I mean, I have a heartbeat. That's good, right?"

"It's not bad. It's how I knew my friends were still alive even without their heads. They were still breathing, still had pulses."

"Cool." Robby flipped through the sketches again. "So I made all this happen?"

Ethan thought about this. Really, he had *been* thinking about this. "I think you put everything you had into this movie. Hopes, dreams, tons of work—so much fake blood and all those props and those sets. And your Mom? She got you that video camera, right? It all meant a lot to you."

Robby blinked back tears. "Mom loved scary movies."

"So I think...when your father destroyed your camera...I mean, I felt something. It was like a flash of lightning, all that emotion, like a tornado or a storm. And when lightning strikes, Frankenstein comes alive."

"Frankenstein was the doctor, not the monster."

Ethan shrugged. "Maybe the doctor *was* the monster."

"Whoa." Robby paused. "So am I the monster and the doctor? What does that make my Dad? Is he the monster?"

"I don't really know. I think the movie is the monster. I think once your dad broke the camera, it unleashed something. Energy or anger or, or, or something. That created the monster, created this place, and I think you're trapped here same as me."

"Is that my real dad? Is he...also trapped here?"

Ethan shrugged. "Again, I don't know, Robby. I don't even know if I'm right about any of this. I'm sorry."

"Yeah, me too." Robby sighed. "So, now what?"

The big question.

The *biggest* question.

Ethan wanted to do the right thing and save his friends and stop the monster, and to do all that...he was pretty sure he had to save Robby.

"You said you weren't Rocky Killdare," Ethan explained. "You said you weren't a director. But that's not true. You created the scariest movie ever made." He held up his sketchbook as demonstration. "You made a *real monster* happen. This stuff? Stories and art and everything? They have power." And as he was saying this, he thought about the teddy bear and the chainsaw and Olivia—his art, almost leaping off the page and making the scene in front of them.

"You okay? Your face just kinda went blank there, kid."

"I am. I am okay. I have an idea." Wait, no. "I have a *plan*." He whipped open the sketchbook, ready to draw.

Robby rubbed his hands together. "Tell me."

"I'll show you. I'll sketch it out. Storyboard-style."

"Nice."

"But. Um. You're not going to like it."

Robby paled.

"We need to summon the monster," Ethan said.

"The monster. You mean—"

Ethan nodded grimly. "Your father."

FORTY-SEVEN
THE PEN IS MIGHTIER THAN THE MONSTER

FLASH.

It happened fast. Ethan didn't expect that. The world went *whoosh* beneath his feet, and the air pulsed with light. Suddenly he was standing back in the driveway, in the midst of Robby's—no, Rocky Killdare's—homemade movie set. All around them were the plywood and the mannequins and the long extension cords. Over there was the teddy bear and the chainsaw. And presiding over it all—

Robby and his father.

His father was in the middle of saying, "And it's messed up that you love it, Robby. The neighbors stare. Your teachers say you're distracted. This isn't healthy. This stuff, these awful *stories*, they're not *healthy*. Nobody wants to be scared, Robby. It's dumb. It's stupid, dumb nonsense and you know it."

"You took something from me," Robby said.

That, a deviation from the script, a script this whole strange realm had been running on for years now, even decades.

And something else was different too—

The sketchbook tucked under Ethan's arm.

Robby's father looked shaken.

He stumbled over his words—

"I—wh—you can't—" And then the man squeezed his eyes shut so hard, Ethan thought he might implode his whole head. He took a deep breath and stammered his way back on-script, responding to words Robby didn't even say this time around. "Your—your *sister* Carrie is leaving for college in the fall. Besides, she's a mess too. She wants to be a—a what, some charity worker—"

"This isn't about Carrie, Dad. This is about me." Robby stood tall, chin up and out, camera at his feet. "I had a thing I loved to do, and Mom gave that to me and you took it away." At that, he picked up his camera.

"You're—you're *weird* and h-horror movies are—"

"I make cool movies. And I think I'm good at it too."

"You'll always fail!"

"You made me a monster! We're both a monster!" Robby said.

And at that, it was time.

Ethan flipped open his sketchbook to a recent page. He tore it loose from its binding and took a deep breath, unsure if this would work—but this was not reality, this was something between a dream and a nightmare. Ethan took a deep breath—

And flipped the sketch through the air, almost like it was a Frisbee.

It spun and fluttered.

And suddenly, almost like a paper tacking itself to a corkboard, it slapped flat against Robby's father's chest, where it became more than just a sketch. Because on that paper, Ethan had drawn a place. And now the sketch was a portal—a hole in reality. It pulled them through it—

Flash.

They were in Kevin Rook's basement.

Screenhead, with its lithe, shadowy limbs, stalked the room.

Its screen turned from a searching eye to a hungry mouth.

It *vwom-vwom-vwommed*, and when it did, Ethan

realized it sounded weirdly like a videotape in Rocky's camera rewinding.

Something was different, though. Not only was the monster there. And the room full of sixth graders. But Robby was there too, defiant. And his father stood the same distance away, watching this all unfold around him.

"You broke something when you broke that camera," Robby said. "You broke my movie. You broke the thing that Mom left me. You broke my dream, *Dad*. Don't you see that?"

Ethan flipped another sketch—*spin, whoosh, flash.*

Again the scene changed.

Now: in town. Screenhead sliding its way through living rooms across the darkened neighborhood. Gobbling power. Eating heads. *Chomp chomp chomp.*

"This is what we became!" Robby yelled.

Ethan threw another sketch.

The scene was now Ethan's living room as Screenhead attacked Janine. He wasn't there when it happened, but it didn't matter—Ethan's imagination was as broad as it was deep, and he brought it to this moment as Janine screamed, her phone still in her hand, the monster descending toward her, its hungry glitch-screen mouth buzzing.

"You did this to us!"

Ethan threw another sketch.

Screenhead had grown massive, arms as big as tractor trailers, body a sliding, serpentine tube. Olivia screaming as it moved to close its giant teeth around her neck.

"It turned me—it turned *us*—into that!" Robby yowled. "And our nightmare became the scariest movie ever made. And now it's loose. In the world!"

Another sketch—

This one, brand-new, from the deepest, darkest recesses of Ethan's imagination...

Flash.

A cityscape. Maybe New York, maybe Philadelphia or San Francisco, Ethan didn't quite know and it didn't quite matter. Robby, his father, and Ethan were standing above it, separate from it—buildings were torn in half. Many on fire. Sirens blared. But the screaming could still be heard above that din.

A great shadow lorded over the city, stalking its streets. Big as any skyscraper now, Screenhead was many-limbed, like something half-human and half-spider. Its mouth, big as ten billboards bolted together, flickered, a widening maw as its greedy arachnid-like limbs fed whole pieces of building into itself. People clung to the sides of destroyed skyscrapers as kaiju-monster Screenhead wolfed them all down like they were just clumps of stuck-together movie popcorn.

It must be said that Ethan was particularly proud of this drawing.

Robby thought of it—

But Ethan drew it.

And it was the best thing he'd ever done.

All the detail. All the shading. The 3D radial lines used to frame out the full shapes of streets and buildings. And now here it was, really for real in front of him, and it didn't scare him at all. It was too cool to scare him. Because he'd made this. *They'd* made this. Together.

Robby said, softer now: "Dad, it's out there. It's out there and it's going to do this. But we can stop it. We can change the script. I can finish my movie my way. You can let me do it this time."

"I...," his father said, looking horror-struck at the ruined cityscape just below them. Screenhead caught a fighter jet in its spidery fingers and chucked it into its flat mouth. It exploded as it went down into the beast's dark gullet.

Robby's father looked all around, and then back to his son—

And then to the camera now in the boy's hand—

His eyes shone with tears.

He blinked them away.

And then the eyes turned red once more.

His father roared and stomped the ground, and Ethan nearly fell down as everything rushed up past him—the buildings, an ambulance, the broken limbs of the shadow monster—and then suddenly they were in the driveway again. Back to where they began.

And Robby's dad stormed forward, snatched up the camera in his hand, raising it above his head—

Ready to throw it down and smash it once more.

FORTY-EIGHT
ONE MORE SKETCH

THANKFULLY, ETHAN HAD DRAWN ONE more sketch, one he'd hidden from Robby.

He pulled it out as Robby's father raised the camera—

And he flipped it toward the man.

It whirled through the air.

And then—

The camera in Robby's father's hand twitched.

Which made the man pause.

"Hnnh?" he asked.

Even Robby looked confused, shooting Ethan a quizzical glance.

But Ethan didn't have time to explain. It would explain itself soon enough.

The camera made a sound—its rewinding sound,

vwom, vwom, vwommmm, louder and louder as it began to shake. The man tried to throw it to the ground now, but it would not be shaken free, oh no, for a pair of sharp-angled arms with far too many joints had thrust out from the sides of the camera, gripping his wrists with a vice-like crush. The man yelped as legs sprouted underneath the camera—and its lens extended out, like a snake—

"Robby! Robby, what have you done!"

"I—" Robby said, looking more and more panicked.

Ethan knew he, too, should've been panicked. This, for him, was absolutely textbook panic time. And yet he felt no such emotion. He just felt—

Well, he felt like, *I made this, I know what this is, and this is right.*

So he gave a small, sad smile and two thumbs-up to Robby.

It's going to be okay, he mouthed to his new friend.

And Robby nodded slowly, surely, and turned back to watch his father be eaten by his video camera.

The camcorder did not gobble him up all at once, though the process was not slow. The front lens became a mouth, less flat and more like a snapping gator's maw—this one made of shadow and glass—and it stretched wide, *too* wide, impossibly so, before closing on the man's head.

It did not stop there. It worked its way down him, one bite after the next, *chomp, munch, crunch,* until all that was left were Robby's father's feet. And then it ate those, too, work boots and all.

At that, the camera—standing tall on the ink-dark stilts of its legs—did a backflip toward Robby. As it spun through the air, its mouth and arms and legs retracted into its camcorder body, just before Robby caught it.

It was just a camera now.

No monster.

No inky-black limbs.

No ever-hungry, all-consuming mouth.

Just...a camera.

"I...," Robby said, clearly flummoxed. He looked to the camera and back to where his father had been standing, then back to the camera. "What happened? Did you—is he—what the—"

"It's over. I think." *I hope.*

"Is my father...dead?"

"I don't think that was really your father, Robby."

Robby blinked. His jaw hung open and he looked around, maybe less scared than he was bewildered. "I think you're maybe right about that." Looking left and right as if something might jump out at him from nowhere, he finally seemed to relax, letting loose a slow sigh of relief. "So. Um. What happens now?"

"I think you get to finish your movie."

"Yeah?"

"Yeah."

"You're going to stay and help me finish it, right?"

Ethan hesitated. "I'd love to. But...I think I have to go home."

"Oh." *Blink, blink*. With more sadness: *"Oh."*

"It's cool. I'll be out there waiting for your movie, okay?"

Robby smiled. "Yeah. Yeah. Okay. You're gonna watch it?"

"I'm gonna watch it."

"You'll watch the first two, right? *Not* the third one. But, like, horror movies in general? You gotta watch the scary movies, kid. You gotta be a little scared sometimes. It's like—it's like a vaccine. You need a little bit of it here and there to help you through the times when it's big, and when it's real."

"I will."

Robby leaned in, eager and excited. "Promise?"

"Promise," Ethan said with a laugh.

At that, Robby threw himself at the other boy,

launching into a hug with the video camera trapped between them. Even though it was boxy and kind of hurt, it was still a good hug. And Ethan didn't even worry about germs during it, which was a huge win.

"Thanks, Ethan."

"No problem, Robby. Now go be Rocky and finish the movie."

They let go of the hug.

And then the world suddenly rushed up past Ethan once more—

Whoosh.

Flash.

And—

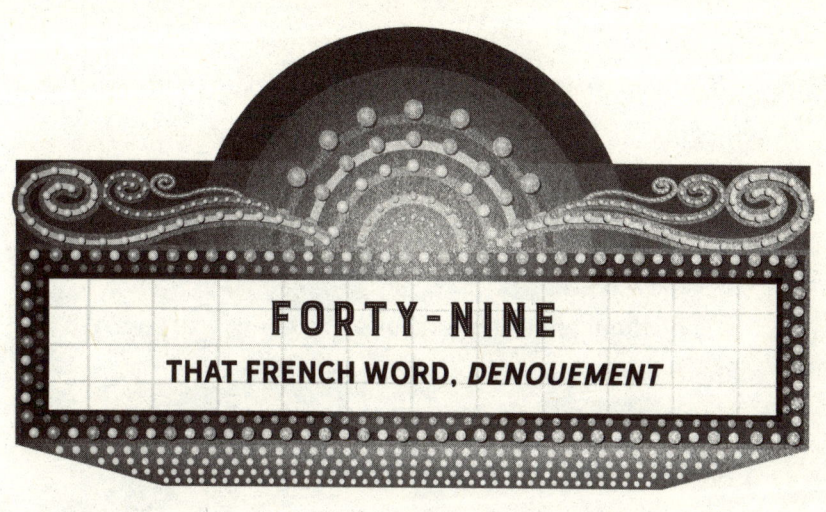

FORTY-NINE
THAT FRENCH WORD, *DENOUEMENT*

FINDING HIMSELF ON A CONCRETE floor and in the dark, Ethan stood up.

He had been sandwiched between rows of seats in an old movie theater. No, *the* old movie theater. The Monarch.

The power was out. The theater was dark. The only lights were from the exit signs at the top of the theater. An eerie red glow permeated.

Nearby: a small *ugggh* sound.

He knew that sound!

"Olivia!" he cried out, reaching down and helping her up.

Her hair was all sideways, and she smoothed out the rumples in her clothing. "Ethan. Dude." She looked around. "Is this—is this the Monarch?"

Oh god. She doesn't remember. She doesn't remember any of it.

"Yes," he said, tentatively.

"Is it gone?"

"It? You mean—"

"The monster, dude! The big, you know, scary-movie monster? Oh, please tell me you remember it."

He exhaled, and in flooded all the relief in the world. "I remember. I promise, I remember. I remember Kevin Rook's, I remember us being here and Evil Abe the Manager, I remember your head getting taken off, you being on that mannequin body, the teddy bear with a chainsaw—"

"Whoa whoa whoa," Olivia said. "What mannequin body? I had my head taken off?? And what do you mean '*teddy bear with a chainsaw*'? Dude. *Dude.*"

"You—you don't remember all of that."

"You are definitely playing."

"I'm not playing."

Under her breath she said, "Then maybe I'm glad I don't remember." But then: "Hey. Where is Evil Abe, anyway?"

At that, one of the exit doors popped open with a *ch-chung*—and someone fled through the doors, escaping. "That was him, I think," Ethan said.

"Good, he better run."

"We don't need to chase him, do we?"

"You wanna chase him? That's not like you."

"If we have to, then we will."

She sighed. "I don't think we're gonna catch that guy, dude. He knows what he did. People like that always get what's coming to them. He's too messy."

"Yeah."

"Can we get out of here?" she asked.

"Definitely."

Outside, the street was dark. But people were already wandering around, looking confused. Doubly so when the power came back on—not all at once, but cascading across the town, from east to west, electricity bringing the light in a wave, as if to banish the darkness.

Olivia and Ethan looked around but didn't see Evil Abe.

He really was gone. For now, at least.

"You good?" Ethan asked her.

"I'm good. You good?"

"I am, actually."

"Thanks, Ethan. I don't know what you did, I don't know how you did it, I don't know what kind of messed-up stuff you saw—but I know you saved us. You. Ethan Pitowski!" She sounded a little shocked, but it felt nice all the same.

They hugged.

Though as it would turn out, she was the only one who knew he'd saved everyone.

Well, her and one other.

FIFTY
ROLL CREDITS?

NOBODY ELSE REMEMBERED WHAT HAD happened that night.

Which was probably a good thing, since pretty much everyone in town literally lost their heads to a TV-headed shadow monster. This was not a thing they recalled—all they knew was, they were okay one minute, then everything went dark, figuratively and literally. They lost consciousness, then woke up again to a power outage, which swiftly resolved.

The adults were confused.

The government called it an "airborne toxic event," claiming that a train had derailed fifty miles away and the wind had moved a mysterious cloud of chemicals over their town—it wasn't enough to cause lasting harm but did cause enough of a reaction to knock everyone out for a little while.

Olivia asked Ethan one day, "Do you think that's possibly what really happened? That it was just a train? Just some, like, funky chemicals?"

"Do *you* think that?" he asked her.

"Nah," she said.

"Me neither."

"Whadda you guys talking about?" Harley asked, bounding up to them after school like a happy-if-bewildered golden retriever.

Ethan shrugged. "Nothing. Just how we didn't suffer from an 'airborne toxic event' last month, and how actually the scariest movie ever made turned into a literal monster and ate off everybody's heads but then we beat the monster and everything was okay again, except nobody remembers what happened but Olivia and me."

Harley laughed. "That's *awesome*. Ethan, you're so creative. I love your stories and your drawings. *Ooh ooh*, you should draw that! Draw it. I know you don't like scary stuff, but c'mon, please. You gotta."

"I like scary stuff okay," Ethan said.

"Yeah, you're different now," Olivia said, eyeing him. "You, like, leveled up or something."

"*Ding*," Ethan said, making the level-up noise. They laughed.

Olivia slugged him on the side of the arm. "Hey, and for real, your art saved our butts. Like, more than once, I think." She didn't—couldn't—remember all of it. But he had told her the whole story. (And thankfully, she believed him. Maybe some part of her *did* remember.)

At that he just shrugged. "Maybe."

"No maybe about it, dude."

"Wish my parents knew that. Wish they *cared* that I want to be an artist." So bad. Real bad. So so real really bad.

"So tell them how much it matters to you," Olivia said.

"And hey, man," Harley said, getting his face all up in Ethan's face. "You don't wanna be an artist."

Ethan's heart sank. "I...don't?"

"Nah, man. 'Cause you already *are* an artist," Harley said as if this idea were blazingly obvious. It hadn't been blazingly obvious to Ethan before. Not even a little bit.

But he was starting to figure it out.

─◆•◆─

At home the next night, Ethan went up to his room, did his homework, then started to draw. Part of him was afraid he wouldn't be able to or wouldn't want to—that somehow it would conjure for him the memories of all that had happened with the movie monster and with Robby. Or worse still, that his art would or could *literally* conjure it—recreating the creature out of nothing but his own mind.

But that doubt, that fear, was there for only a moment.

A speed bump, not a roadblock.

So onward he went, drawing his memories of all that had happened, lost to the reverie of it. Humming to himself and smiling and chewing his lip as he sometimes did when he really, really got down to it.

Eventually his father came into his room.

"Let's put that away now, Ethan," Dad said, the sour note of disappointment in his voice. Like the bleat from an ill-trained trombonist.

"Okay," Ethan said quietly. But his hand froze.

He did not put it away.

His dad said nothing.

He said nothing either.

"Ethan—"

"I did all my homework."

"That's good. But—"

"And I even got the problems right in math." *I think.*

"Wonderful, it's just—remember what we talked about."

"Yeah." Ethan lowered his head. "I know, it's just—" He bit his tongue again. *Do it. Say it. Speak it aloud. Or better yet...* "Here."

He thrust the sketchbook toward his father.

Dad looked at it like it was a dead squirrel. And he took it the same way, almost as if it might come alive at any moment and bite him.

He began slowly, almost meticulously, turning the pages. The man paused at each, his face growing all the more dour and dire and dark with every one. A cloud moving in front of the sun.

He hates it, Ethan thought, his heart falling in his chest. But the sadness of that gave way to something else: a kind of anger, a thrust of pride.

And the words tumbled out without him even thinking. One minute he was feeling pent-up, and the next, his truth was *spoken into the world*.

"Dad, I'm very good at drawing, but it doesn't even matter if I'm really good or not, because it's the thing I love and so it's the thing I want to do. I don't know if it's the thing I'm going to do with the rest of my life or not, because I'm too young to make that kind of plan, but I *do* know you do the thing you love to do so I should be allowed to do the thing I love to do, and you can't stop me from doing it. You can throw my sketchbook in the trash, and I will draw on the walls if I have to—and if you throw my pens away or my colored pencils, I will find a rock outside and draw on the sidewalk—"

"Son—"

"—because, Dad, this is who I am, I'm an artist, and an artist is a person who makes art and you can't stop me, and *trust me* when I say it's a bad idea to try—"

"*Son.*"

"—and I know you think I'm going to get, I dunno, attacked by a goose and not be able to pay my rent, but I swear—"

"Son!"

That time, spoken with volume and urgency. Two rare things for his father.

"Um. What?" Ethan's heart thudded in his chest. He was scared suddenly. Which felt weirder to him than it used to—maybe because of how often he *wasn't* scared these days. Huh.

"These are"—Dad blinked—"amazing."

"You just don't underst—" *Understand me*, Ethan was about to say, but *whoa*, hold up, slow down, what had his father just said? *"Amazing?"* No, no, he couldn't have said that. He must have said *crazying* or...or...*poorly appraising*, or maybe he was just about to say *amazingLY HORRIBLE* and Ethan just hadn't let him finish. He paused. But his father said no more. "Did you say '*amazing*'?"

"I did. These are like...well...These are like some of the comic books I read growing up. They're really something, kiddo."

"Something bad?"

"No." His father chuckled. "Hon!" he called suddenly into the other room. "Come in here. You need to see these!" Mom came hurrying into the room looking panicked, because she was probably sure that something was on fire or there were bees or something. Her favorite question was the one she asked right now:

"What's the matter?"

But Dad just tilted the sketchbook toward her. He turned the pages.

Her eyes widened. Her mouth formed the same O shape as when you were watching fireworks.

"Oh, sweetheart. Look at these. Wouldja just look at these. They sure are something special." She turned to Ethan. "You drew them?"

"Yeah."

And at that they sat with him and looked at his work together. They told him they loved it and had had no idea what he could do with those pens and pencils. He told them he hadn't had any idea either until recently—though on that point they'd never really understand, because how could he ever really tell them everything?

Mom went back to the kitchen to keep cooking dinner, and Dad lingered for a moment. He knelt down and put a hand on Ethan's shoulder. "You are good at this. And you'll only get better if you keep practicing. It'll take work. And the world will be harder for you than for other people, maybe. Or...maybe not. You really are impressive, Ethan. Even if I don't...understand you all the time."

He nodded and smiled a little.

"Thanks, Dad."

"Just promise me one thing?"

"Okayyyyy."

"Keep a good head on your shoulders, okay?"

Ethan blinked.

He laughed nervously.

He knew what his father meant but, *uhhh*.

(Screenhead flashed into his mind, chasing him down the hallway after gobbling heads. Yellow teeth and a sinister eye as it scurried closer and closer.)

"The plan is *definitely* to keep my head," Ethan said, smiling.

"Love you, son."

"Love you, Dad."

His father lowered his voice and said, almost conspiratorially, "Just watch out for geese, though. Seriously. It's not a joke. Geese can really hurt you. I found out it's not just their *bites*. They have hard, bony wings and they can—" Dad mimed a goose attack. "You know, it's like a karate chop almost. Goose karate."

"Watch out for geese and their karate."

"Exactly."

"Will do, Dad. Will do."

EPILOGUE
ONE OF THOSE POST-CREDITS SCENES

THEY NEVER FOUND EVIL ABE, the Monster-Unleashing Manager.

One of the few people who probably remembered more than everyone else, he disappeared from the Monarch Theater and ran.

Kevin Rook also left the week after The Event. His parents were in fact getting divorced, and he was going to live with one of them in the city. On Kevin's last day, he went up to Ethan and said, "Hey, I'm sorry I was such a jerkweed. You were pretty cool back there in town. And I'm glad you didn't get your head eaten."

"So you remember what happened."

Kevin fidgeted. "I remember what I did, if that's what you mean."

It *was* what Ethan meant. At least a little. But Kevin had been through enough, hadn't he? "I just mean—you know. Most people don't remember. Just you and me, and Olivia remembers some of it," Ethan told him. "I'm glad you got your head back."

"Yeah, well, see ya."

"See ya."

For the next month, Kevin's desk in the back of the room sat empty.

Until one day, when their homeroom teacher, Mrs. van Eekhout, announced that they were getting a new student.

And then she introduced Robby Kelley, a boy with longish dark hair that curled around his ears.

A boy in a *Death Fingers* T-shirt.

A boy who looked right at Ethan and said, as he walked past him toward his desk, "Hey, kid, I hear you like scary movies too." He chuckled and kept moving.

Ethan didn't understand how this was possible or what was happening, only that he had a lot of questions. A *lot* of questions. But the most important one was:

When could they make a movie?

FIN

ACKNOWLEDGMENTS

I was once afraid of scary movies.

(I was once afraid of lots and lots of things, really. Ethan isn't me, but Ethan definitely contains parts of me. Robby is too, I suppose, and Olivia, and Harley, but such is the nature of the characters—I suspect all my characters contain some portion of me, big or small.)

I was not scared *by* scary movies individually—I mean, that's their job, to scare you. I was scared by them *as a group*, as a whole phenomenon. Scared not just of seeing one but scared because they existed at all in the world. And this fear is in part because of one movie:

The Exorcist.

It's not a movie for middle graders, just so we're clear—but when I was that age, *your* age, most likely, my sister (who is eleven years older than me) had seen the movie and regaled me with tales of how Truly Terrifying it was. As in, people watched the movie and—as with *Death Fingers*—basically exploded in fear: bodily fluids spraying everywhere, deafening screaming, heart attacks, comas, the heat-death of the universe, and so forth.

Now, none of this happened in front of my sister, I don't think, and I'm guessing she was just telling me the tales *she* had heard from other people—an urban legend passed down, or *creepypasta*. But it was enough to truly freak me out about horror movies as an entire *thing*. I became sure that the most horrifying thing about a horror movie was that it could, I dunno, *make you go crazy and barf and have your brain explode* or something. It wouldn't just scare you, I feared. It would straight up make you die. It was, itself, kind of a monster. It wasn't enough that I could simply avoid watching it. I was afraid it would find me. I was afraid that I'd turn on the TV one day to watch cartoons and instead, it'd be *The Exorcist*. Like it would be waiting for me there in the dark or in the static. Just knowing it was *out there* freaked me out.

Which is where the idea for this book came from.

So I suspect I owe my sister Tracy thanks—also because she put the first horror novel I ever read in my hand when I was an early teen. And I owe my mother (now passed, sadly) thanks for accidentally letting me rent *Alien* thinking it was a fun Star Wars-y sci-fi movie and not what it actually is: a chest-bursting horror movie set in space. It terrified me and I loved it and it was then that I came to enjoy scary stories going forward. Yes, even *The Exorcist*.

Thanks especially to my editor, Deirdre, and my agent, Stacia, for letting this book grow arms and legs and become the shadowy monster it needed to be. Thanks above all must go to the readers of this book and also the readers of my other middle grade novel, *Dust & Grim*, because without that book, I don't know that this one gets to exist. Books are good. Horror is fun. Hope none of you lost your heads while reading this story.

Michelle Wendig

CHUCK WENDIG

is the author of the *New York Times* bestseller *Dust & Grim*, as well as numerous *New York Times*, *USA Today*, and *Los Angeles Times* best-selling novels for adults and young adults. He invites you to find him online at terribleminds.com.